THE

Celia Fremlin
School for Gi
Oxford. During
Mass Observation archives. She began her
writing career in the Fifties and her first novel,
The Hours Before Dawn, was awarded an Edgar
by the Mystery Writers of America. Celia
Fremlin's most recent thriller is *Dangerous
Thoughts*, which is published to coincide with
the first paperback publication of *The Spider-
Orchid* and *Appointment with Yesterday*.

THE SPIDER-ORCHID

by

Celia Fremlin

GOLLANCZ CRIME

Gollancz Crime is an imprint of Victor Gollancz Ltd
14 Henrietta Street, London WC2E 8QJ

First published in Great Britain 1977
by Victor Gollancz Ltd

First Gollancz Crime edition 1991

A CIP catalogue record for this book
is available from the British Library

ISBN 0-575-05089 6

Printed and bound in Great Britain
by Cox & Wyman Ltd, Reading

CHAPTER I

"DARLING, WE'RE TOGETHER at last!" cried Rita, shaking the rain from her hair and spilling a suitcase, a bulging plastic carrier bag, and a clanking tangle of metal coat-hangers into the circle of lamplight at his feet. "*Together!* In our very own home!"

My very own home, Adrian found himself thinking uncontrollably, even while he folded her in his arms, murmuring into her ear all the appropriate words of welcome. *My* flat. *Mine*. And now the woman I love is moving into it, bag and baggage, and there is nothing in the wide world I can do to stop it, because it was my idea.

"If only we could be together *always!*" he'd said to her, not once but dozens of times over the past four years. Had said it, and had meant it.

But of course, he'd never thought for one moment that it would ever actually happen.

Aloud he said:

"Yes, darling, marvellous! I can still hardly believe it's really happening. . . ."

This, at least, was the truth. As with any major shock, his mind was refusing to take in, all at one go, the full enormity of the situation; it was letting the realisation get to him a little bit at a time, inch by inch, as much as his shrinking spirit could bear.

The plastic bag of groceries? He could face that. She often brought food when she came for the evening. The suitcase? That, too, was not totally unfamiliar; they had been away together occasionally. But the coat-hangers. . . ? His eye slid past them as if they were a nasty street-accident piled up on the side of the road. He couldn't, wouldn't, just yet, take in their terrible implications—the dreadful glittering threat they posed to the very core of his comfortable, self-sufficient existence. His imagination simply blocked out, it refused, as yet, to envisage his well-pressed suits, his jackets, trousers and ties relegated to the darkest recesses of the wardrobe; squeezed back and back, in helpless retreat before

the victorious tide of dresses, blouses, fur jackets, matching hand-
bags, platform sandals, knee-length boots . . . the lot.

And that would only be the beginning. Already he could see her
eyes darting round the room, altering things, getting rid of things,
planning where *her* things were to go.

"Marvellous, darling," he repeated, as if he had learned the
words by rote and was checking that he'd got them right. "Marvellous! I think this calls for a little celebration, don't you?"

Diving into the drinks cupboard by the fireplace, he tried to
compose his face a little before facing her again.

"Well, cheers, darling!" he heard himself saying a minute later.
"To us!" And as they touched glasses, his neat whisky against
her gin and tonic, he found himself staring not into Rita's sloe-
dark, expectant eyes, but into the shining yellow liquid in his
glass. How long, he was desperately wondering, could the drink
be made to last? Because once the drinking was over, then the
thing would really have to start.

Drinking to future happiness is one thing; embarking on it
quite another.

"Darling, I'm so happy!" cried Rita, as she had every right to
do: and, "Darling, so am I!" he responded, with an awful sinking
of the stomach. Over the glittering rim of the whisky, he fixed his
eyes on the black, springy hair through which his fingers had so
often ruffled; on the white, untroubled brow which had once seemed
to betoken such serenity of spirit; and he tried to feel the old,
melting enchantment. But all he could feel was a sort of sick
paralysis of the will; a sense of having lost control over his own
life; the helpless terror of one who has sold his soul to . . .

What an unfair and terrible thought! Anyone less like the devil
than Rita, with her pale, oval face, her big, pathetic eyes and
tremulous mouth, it would be difficult to imagine. "Angel" would
have been a fairer comparison—especially now, with that halo
of raindrops round her hair . . . and only now did he realise, with
compunction, that he had not yet invited her to take her coat off.
She was sitting there, sipping gin and tonic, in wet shower-proof
nylon.

"Darling, your coat . . . I'm so sorry!" he exclaimed, leaning
over the back of the settee and slipping it from her shoulders. "It's
soaking, I'll just . . ."

He stopped, brought up short as if by a sudden blow. The coat *belonged* here now. No good just throwing it over the rack in the bathroom to dry off in time for her to go home. She wasn't going home. The coat was going to live here. There would have to be a place for it, a peg in the hall allotted to it. *Its* peg.

For several seconds Adrian just stood there, like a man in shock, the limp, damp, rust-coloured thing hanging over his arm like a dead animal, trophy of a hunt now disbanded.

"I'll just . . . hang it up," he muttered; and when he came back into the living-room he poured himself another whisky, holding it up against the light, screwing his eyes up as if to enjoy the golden radiance of it.

How the *hell* did I get into this, he was asking himself. How the hell *did* I?

But of course, he knew the answer. Knew, too, that it was no use blaming Rita. Even this morning—even in those first awful moments of hearing her babbling the glorious news down the telephone before he'd even had his breakfast—even then, he'd recognised that the blame was not hers. Those awful feelings that rose in his gorge as he listened to her ecstatic chatter were his, and his alone. Not her fault at all.

"Darling, you'll *never* guess!" she'd cried excitedly; but of course he'd guessed at once, guessed without any shadow of doubt, taken aback only by the violence of his own dismay. He had no *right* to be dismayed, absolutely no right at all, he should have been over the moon with joy, because what she was doing was only what he had asked her to do—begged her, indeed—over and over again during the long, happy years when it was impossible. They'd agreed long ago—agreed jointly, and without acrimony or argument—that if only Derek would agree to a divorce, then she'd come and live with Adrian.

And now, this very day, Derek *had* agreed. In the first shock of hearing the news, Adrian had felt, for a moment, as if he had been betrayed by his dearest friend.

Which was ridiculous. He and Derek Langley had only met a couple of time in all these years, both times, naturally, in the role of enemies. In the circumstances, there was no other role open to them.

Which was a pity, in a way, for Adrian had felt no hostility at

7

all to Derek as a person. In fact, he had rather liked him; the sensation he remembered most clearly from that first encounter had been one of vague, foolish gratitude towards the man for being nearly a decade older than himself, with grey, thinning hair and gold-rimmed bifocals. It had seemed to simplify things; and though, in fact, the assumption was to prove illusory, Adrian still retained in his recollections the pleasant sense of easy superiority it had engendered in him at the time. The ensuing conversation had, in the nature of things, been somewhat prickly and uncomfortable; but Adrian had nevertheless formed a mildly favourable impression of his rival. Derek Langley seemed a quiet, inoffensive sort of man, sensible and well-balanced, and with an intriguingly expert knowledge of wild flowers in Britain. Few subjects could be more remote from Adrian's own special interests, but all the same, Adrian liked expertise in no matter what sort of field; liked and admired it, and recognised it when he saw it.

In happier circumstances—or perhaps one should say less dramatic ones—he and Derek could have been friends; but of course in their respective roles of importunate lover and outraged husband, this would never have done.

The second time they'd met had been some months later, on a grey January afternoon just after Adrian's own divorce had been successfully completed.

"But she loves me! You *can't* stand in the way of her happiness like this!" Adrian remembered declaiming; and, "Can't I? Just you watch," Derek had countered placidly, and had gone on sticking labels on to his colour slides, licking and placing each one in position with careful accuracy.

"But that's just possessiveness!" Adrian recalled himself protesting—he remembered that the winter afternoon light was already fading in Derek's quiet, book-lined study. And Derek had nodded his head thoughtfully, agreeing that Yes, it probably was just possessiveness: he was rather a possessive sort of person, actually.

It had seemed like deadlock. Adrian had raged, Rita had sobbed, and Derek had gone on preparing his talk for the Annual General Meeting of the West Midlands Botanical Society; and it presently emerged—though when or how such a decision had been reached Adrian could never clearly recall—that Poor Derek mustn't be upset; he would come round in his own time, but meantime Rita mustn't do anything nasty to him, like leaving him for another man, or neglecting to be home in time to cook his supper.

Naturally, Adrian had at the time fought this rather unadventurous programme with all the fervour that becomes an impassioned lover: but actually, in the end, it had all worked out rather well, with Rita arriving at two o'clock on Thursday afternoons to go to bed with him, and taking herself away promptly at four because of Poor Derek. Sometimes, she came on Tuesday evenings as well and cooked a meal for Adrian; or maybe they'd go to the theatre together, but she was always gone well before midnight because of Poor Derek, and so Adrian was able to get to bed at his usual time. He hated being kept up late; it triggered off in him a tiresome kind of insomnia that kept him half-awake, half-dreaming for the best part of the night, leaving him depressed and irritable, and quite unfit for the pressures and demands of his job the next day. Poor Derek, it seemed, suffered a similar problem, that's why Rita had to be home so promptly by midnight. They made a singularly compatible triangle, Adrian sometimes reflected; they could hardly have been luckier in one another.

How comfortable it had all been, he mused now, staring disconsolately into the golden depths of the whisky. How secure, and settled, and unbothersome! Even the yearnings and the frustrations, he realised now, had been an integral part of the happiness.

"Oh, if only you didn't have to *go*, darling," he'd so often sighed, as the hands of the bedside clock crept onward, and Rita began to fidget, and look for her stockings, and think about trains to Wimbledon; "Oh, if only you could stay with me longer . . . all night. . . ."

Actually, it would have been most inconvenient if she'd stayed all night: not because anyone else in the house would have objected—least of all the landlady—but simply because staying all night necessarily involved still being there in the morning, and this Adrian would have found it hard to tolerate. At forty-seven, a divorced man, and already four years away from the turmoil of family life, Adrian had developed a number of small habits which he himself recognised as old-maidish, but nevertheless had no intention of relinquishing—and foremost among these was his rigid early-morning routine. Up at seven—long, leisurely bath, followed by yoghurt, cornflakes, egg boiled for an exact four minutes—and all the time a book propped in front of him—on the

9

soapdish, alongside the bathroom mirror, or leaning against the coffee-pot while he ate. And there was the silence, too, the sense of unassailable solitude. Lovely, enveloping solitude, from which he could emerge unscathed into his busy day like a moth from its cocoon.

All of which was completely incompatible with Rita. Why he was so sure of this, Adrian would have found it hard to say, since he had never given her a trial; but he just knew.

And now, through no fault of his own—unless letting things slide, taking each day as it came, were to be counted as faults— now, the whole thing was to be whipped from under his feet, without warning or apology. Whipped away not just for a single morning—and even *that* prospect had, in the past, been enough to put him on his guard—but for *all* his mornings, for the rest of the foreseeable future.

Rita not wanting to be woken as early as seven ... Rita in the bathroom ... Rita saying why not shredded wheat? ... Rita boiling his egg too soft, or, as the case might be, too hard. ...

That Rita would take over these and similar housewifely concerns, despite any protests that Adrian might nerve himself to make, was a virtual certainty. She (like any other woman in her position) would know that she had just so long to make herself indispensable to him, and so she would set about it without delay, burrowing like a frantic woodworm into the structural framework of his life in order, with a touch here and a touch there, to make sure that the previously smooth-running machinery would no longer work without her. The organising of his breakfast would undoubtedly be one of her first projects; she would appropriate it to herself with all speed, and, simple though Adrian's routine might sound, and carefully as he might explain it to her, she would inevitably get it subtly wrong.

His fault this, of course, for being so pernickety; but nevertheless, she would.

The reading, of course, would be the first thing to go: the delicious habit of reading non-stop while he ate, while he bathed, while he shaved. During the four years he had been on his own, he had solved one by one all the minor practical problems attendant upon such a habit, even the problem of his reading glasses steaming up in the bath. Now, just when there was no little annoyances left at all, *this* had to happen!

Of course, no woman could be expected to put up with this sort of thing, morning after morning; or, if she could, then the un-remitting consciousness of her sitting there putting up with it would have been every bit as disturbing as outright nagging.

So the reading would have to go. He would have to give it up, as people give up smoking, and with the same sense of outrage and disorientation. There was no way of conveying to any woman— least of all one who loved him—the intensity of his need for that lovely, self-absorbed interlude before he set out to face the day; an interlude of absolute peace in the company of non-judgemental, non-existent characters for whose problems he, Adrian, was in no way to blame.

Oh, those blissfully undemanding murders! Those cosy scenes of blackmail and kidnapping, whose double-crossing implications were all going to be sorted out by rival spy-rings without the smallest reference to him! How soothing they were, to a busy man! He even read science fiction at times, and whole galaxies could blow up without him having to stir a finger. . . !

"Darling! You're in a *trance*!"

With a pink-varnished finger-nail—she must have done them specially before coming here, right in the middle of the final scene with Derek—Rita reached over and flicked him playfully under the chin. She laughed as she did it, a bit too merrily, showing all her little white teeth with practically no fillings, and asked him what his plans were for the evening?

Plans? From now on, was he going to have to have *plans?*

"We must *celebrate*, darling!" she explained gaily. "We must do something *wonderful* with our first—our *very first*— evening. . . !"

It wasn't as wonderful as all that; but he hoped she hadn't noticed; that for her, maybe, it had all been fine.

As, indeed, he pretended it had been for him.

Isn't it marvellous not having to keep an eye on the *time*, they kept saying to each other, as they lay, afterwards, in the big bed.

Not having to get dressed . . . go out . . . say good-bye to one another. Marvellous, they kept saying. . . Marvellous.

He could tell that Rita knew that something was wrong; and that she knew that he knew. He knew, too, that she would never bring herself to ask him what it was; she was too afraid of the answer. And so was he.

CHAPTER II

OF COURSE, IF he had thought to look back at the long-drawn-out trauma of his own divorce, at the actual day-to-day mechanics of breaking a marriage of fairly long standing, Adrian would have realised that his panic over Rita's sudden arrival had been premature. He would have recollected that someone rushing out of the house with a suitcase rarely heralds the end of the partnership. Within forty-eight hours, the runaway partner is usually slinking uneasily back again, feeding the cat, collecting laundry, leaning over the fence to put the neighbours right about the awful lies that Partner B has been feeding them these last two days.

And then—since by this time it is gone seven, and Partner B has arrived home from work—a meal is guardedly improvised, and over the take-away curry and the tinned apricots, the battle-weary pair check through their new haul of grievances, measuring them against the old, blending and interweaving them so skilfully that within an hour or two this latest outrage has become virtually indistinguishable from all the rest. Forgotten wedding anniversaries ... nights spent out on the landing in tears ... the awful things *he* said ... the horrible things *she* said.... Before either of them quite realise what's happening, everything has slithered impercept-ibly back to square one, and it is as if she (or he) had never slammed out of the house yesterday (or the day before) at all.

Rita's experience, it seemed, was to be no exception. Far from worrying herself about Adrian's boiled egg, or otherwise making herself indispensable, she was on the phone to her husband before eight in the morning; by quarter past, she was repacking her suitcase, albeit tearfully, and borrowing a pound for her taxi fare. Poor Derek, it seemed, had omitted to consult his diary and remind her, when she walked out on him, of all the various engagements which she must now either cancel or else turn round and walk back in again for: chief among which was the party they were sup-posed to be giving on the twenty-fifth for Rita's mother's seven-tieth birthday. It was unthinkable that Mummy, who had been so against the marriage in the first place, should be allowed now to guess that anything had gone wrong; and so they'd have to go through with the celebration, candles and all, *seventy* of them! The party wasn't until Friday, but there was all the shopping to do, Rita explained, and the fillings for the fruit flans, and blanching the almonds ... not to mention cleaning and polishing the whole house so that Mummy wouldn't start about velveteen being a dust-trap before she'd even opened her presents. ...

Yes, said Adrian, trying to keep the relief out of his voice. Yes, he quite understood, it was a shame, darling, but never mind, I'll be all right, you concentrate on giving the old lady a good time. ... Already, his eyes were straying hungrily to his book, he kept waiting for the taxi to arrive, for Rita to stop running from room to room, for her to be actually *gone*, so that he could settle down to his second cup of coffee in peace and solitude. It was amazing how many reasons she found for scuttling in and out, the door banging open and shut behind her, where's my bag, have you seen my cigarettes, phone me well before six in case Poor Derek ...

But at last it was over.

"Good-bye, darling!" she cried, for the third or fourth time, while the taxi, its engine switched on, muttered impatiently at the kerbside, nibbling away at Adrian's pound. "Good-bye, it's only for a few days, I'll be back by Sunday. ..."

"*Sunday*! Oh *no*. ..."

With any luck, she hadn't heard. The tactless words had burst from his lips quite uncontrollably, as if a rock had fallen on his toe. *Sunday*!

Of course, she would have to be told some time; but not just now, not like this. He should have broken it to her gently, tactfully, long before the issue became urgent. He should have raised the topic tenderly, understandingly, preferably when she was already lying limp and acquiescent in his arms. "Darling," he should have said, kissing her face, her hair, while he spoke, "darling, it's like this. Sunday is the only day in the whole week when ... well, the thing is, it's a rather special day for me and Amelia. ..."

Or maybe he should approach it the other way round? Maybe he should try and explain to *Amelia* why it was that Rita would henceforth have to share their Sundays? "This friend of mine," he'd say, as casually as he could, "I think I've mentioned her

14

before—her name's Rita, and I'm sure you and she are going to get on famously—well, from now on when you come on Sundays, Rita will be...."

No!

The violence of his rejection took even Adrian himself by surprise. He stood on the front steps actually trembling while the taxi disappeared round the end of the road; then he turned, and made his way back up the three flights of stairs, his mind boiling with a sort of directionless fury, raging against this predicament of his own making.

Rita *mustn't* come here on Sunday, she *mustn't*! Whatever the cost in tears, scenes and accusations, he must keep Rita away. Sunday was sacred to Amelia (yes, sacred; this is sometimes the only word that will do, even for a hard-bitten atheist like Adrian), and he wasn't going to curtail or postpone or modify in the very smallest degree the routine of Amelia's visits, not for anyone in the whole wide world.

Strange that it should have taken a divorce, and all the attendant rows and miseries, to teach him to know his own daughter. Amelia had been nine at the time, and as remote from him, at that age, as if she had been dropped from Mars. It wasn't that she was a particularly difficult little girl, or naturally withdrawn: it was just that she never seemed to talk to *him*. Adrian quickly realised that this was his problem, not hers; she was talkative enough with everyone else, chattering away with her mother, and with her school-friends, too, when they came to tea. He would hear them shrieking and giggling, shrill as parrots, through a thickness of two doors, while he sat in his study, trying to work. In fact, the noise could be frightful, but he was afraid to yell at her, to let himself go, as many fathers would, because he didn't understand her well enough, and knew he didn't. It would have been like tinkering heavy-handedly with a machine of whose purpose and workings he knew nothing.

So quite often, he would take it out on Peggy. What sort of a mother are you? Can't you control that kid ever? It's like living in a madhouse. *Other* mothers manage to . . .

Other mothers, *other* mothers, *what* other mothers? I'm sick to death of hearing about all these Mrs-Bloody-Perfects, you should

15

drop in at Jean's some Saturday afternoon, or the Drapers come to that, *then* you can talk to me about a madhouse! I suppose you'd like your daughter never to speak at all, you'd like her to be autistic, you'd like to have her incapable of making relationships with her peers and trailing off to Child Guidance all the time, like Maureen's wretched brat! That's "Other mothers" for you, why didn't you marry Maureen if that's the sort of thing you want? And she has eczema, too, in case you're interested. . . .

Peggy hadn't always been like this; when he'd married her, she'd been equable and easy-going to a fault. But during that last year before they'd separated, she'd acquired the skills of a fishwife, and almost anything would set her off. Thus he only had to suggest that his daughter should be taught to lower her voice a bit, and there he'd be in the middle of a full-blown scene about Maureen Denvers, when already it wasn't Maureen at all, never had been really, already it was Rita, or beginning to be. But since Peggy didn't even know of Rita's existence at that stage, she'd really had no excuse for staging such a scene; no excuse, certainly, for storming out of the room in a jealous huff and telling Amelia that Daddy was in an awful temper and so she'd have to stop the game and send her little friends home immediately. It was difficult enough being a Daddy, Adrian reflected wearily, without this sort of thing.

Not that Amelia ever seemed to bear any grudges.

"What, Daddy?" she'd say, detached and uncomprehending, when he tried, as he sometimes did, to clear up these misunderstandings; to explain that Mummy had over-stated his complaints, and that he'd never intended actually to stop them playing their game.

Playing what game? Stopped who? Which tea-time? Who did? Amelia never seemed to remember a thing about the episode by the next morning, or even later the same evening, and so Adrian couldn't even apologise and earn the child's forgiveness. Apology and forgiveness are perhaps not the ideal foundation for a father-daughter relationship, but at least they are something. Without them, there was nothing.

It wasn't as if Adrian hadn't tried. The idea of fatherhood, in the abstract, had thrilled him right from the beginning. He could think of no more fascinating hobby than the observing, at first-hand, of the miraculous unfolding of a young mind, the flowering under one's very eyes of a new and unique personality.

16

But it is only fascinating, of course, if the process *does* take place under one's very eyes, and in the case of Adrian and his daughter, this was not so. From her earliest babyhood, all Amelia's flowering, unfolding and the rest had taken place under the eyes of her mother, while Adrian, locked at a mysterious distance, had looked on, at first with painful jealousy, and then, later, with a growing irritation towards both of them. Sometimes—and no doubt this was an outcome of his scientific training—he would set himself to analyse the problem as he would have analysed a recalcitrant chemical in his laboratory, summarising the available data and making inferences from it. Listening, with a twist of pain in his heart, to the easy, intimate exchanges between Amelia and her mother, the relaxed laughter they shared, he would try to analyse, gesture by gesture, exactly what it was that Peggy was doing, and how it differed from what he himself intermittently tried to do.

But it was no good; and as Amelia grew older, and shriller, and no longer wanted to know if octopuses can catch colds or how high a giraffe would be if it stood on the highest mountain in the world, then the thing became even more hopeless. It seemed that the harder he tried, the more painstakingly he sought ways of relating to this skinny, enigmatic being with the thin strands of greasy hair falling into its eyes, the worse was the trouble into which he was liable to flounder. The frustration, the humiliation, and the sheer disappointment of these occasions was hard to endure.

A passionate lover of books himself, he had at first watched, with tremulous optimism, the beginnings of a similar passion in his little daughter; and sometimes, greatly daring, he had nerved himself to read aloud to her from one or other of his own childhood favourites. But if he had hoped that these occasional bedtime sessions might form the foundation of a shared enthusiasm, he was to be disappointed. Amelia would lie there, neat and attentive under her bright blankets, and: "Say thank you to Daddy, darling!" Peggy would admonish, almost before he'd enunciated the last sentence of the story; and from his wife's tone of voice he'd know straight away that he'd done it again: he'd chosen something too babyish ("you can't expect a schoolgirl of nearly ten to bother with *Beatrix Potter*") or too adult ("Rider Haggard is for *teenagers*, dear, you can't expect a little girl of only nine . . .")

And he didn't expect it. Not any longer. Apart from a vague,

17

theoretical satisfaction at having discharged a recognised parental duty, he expected absolutely nothing from these sessions.

And playing with Amelia was even worse. Sometimes the game in question—Snap it might be, or Ludo—would seem, superficially, to be well within the capacities of a professional man at the height of his intellectual powers: but this was an illusion. No sooner did he join in, than the fun would go out of the game, and the mother-daughter rapport would shrivel as if he'd poured poison on it. They'd go on playing, of course, dutifully, and then either he'd win, and feel guilty at having used his highly-trained adult intelligence to score off so small a child, or else he'd lose, and they'd both chide him for not "playing the game".

"It's no *fun*, Daddy, unless you really *try*!" Amelia would protest indignantly, and Peggy would add, gathering up the cards repressively as she spoke: "Yes, Adrian, it *is* humiliating the way you always play to lose! It's so patronising! Children have their pride, you know. . . ." and she'd tell Amelia that it was bedtime, in a tight sort of voice that made it perfectly clear that it *wouldn't* have been bedtime if only Daddy hadn't come along and mucked up the evening.

And so when the divorce, after all the threats, the false starts, the short-lived reconciliations, finally became a reality, Adrian felt quite stunned by how little he minded giving up Amelia. Other fathers weren't like that. All around him, marriages among his and Peggy's acquaintances had been disintegrating, and always the central lament, the battle-cry of both parties, the stone wall against which all other factors beat themselves into insignificance, had been The Children. *I'm* keeping the children. On no account am I letting *her* take the children. I won't give them up, he/she won't give them up, neither of us will give them up.

And now here was Adrian not only willing to give up Amelia, but even, in the secret depths of his heart, actually relieved at the idea of doing so. What sort of a father was he? What sort of an unnatural monster?

And then, after all this—after all the guilt, and the heart-searchings, and the court orders, and the sadness—after all this, it turned out that he hadn't lost Amelia at all, not even in the most mundane and down-to-earth sense. On the contrary, it seemed that he was hereafter expected to spend more time in her exclusive company than he had ever done in his life before—"reasonable access", the courts called it, and what it meant, in plain English, was that he was to collect Amelia at 2.00 pm every Sunday, and take her out somewhere, do something with her, single-handed, until her bedtime some five or six hours later.

Adrian was terrified, as only a man who is really hopeless with children *can* be terrified. The night before the first of these ordeals, he lay awake, sweating. What did she like doing? Where could he take her? What was she interested in? What would he do if she wanted to go to the lavatory and there wasn't one? And there would no longer be Peggy there, telling him he was doing it all wrong, and thereby lifting the responsibility from his shudderingly incompetent shoulders. There would be nothing and nobody, just himself and Amelia, tongue-tied, adrift in uncharted wastelands of measureless embarrassment.

In the end, it wasn't quite as bad as he'd envisaged.

"Hullo, Daddy," Amelia would say, matter-of-factly, often following it up with, "Daddy, can I have. . . ?" "Daddy, will you give me. . . ?"—which were as good ice-breakers as any. Also, she seemed perfectly capable of locating a Ladies for herself and taking herself thither without assistance. As Sunday succeeded Sunday that first winter, he took her to the Zoo, to Madame Tussaud's, to the various museums; and though she was bored, and he was bored, none of it was actually excruciating; indeed, after a while, their mutual boredom began to seem like a faint sort of embryonic link between them, the first he had ever experienced with his own child. He even felt, at times, a perverse little stab of pride at this shared intensity of boredom. Like father, like daughter, he'd find himself thinking with satisfaction as they stumped glumly home from these outings, hardly speaking, thankful, both of them, that it was safely over for one more week.

Still, it couldn't go on like this indefinitely. Adrian's store of patience was far from inexhaustible, and besides, he was getting behind with his work. Sunday had always been his big day for catching up on the technical journals and for assembling his thoughts for the coming week, and so he couldn't go on frittering away valuable time for ever, even for Amelia's sake. He thought, irritably, of the peaky, bored little face between the two skimpy, scraped-back plaits . . . recalled the dragging squeak of her sandals traversing acre after acre of polished floor as they trailed around this or that repository of priceless treasures.

"I *hate* marvels!" he heard a little boy of about six complaining tearfully in the Science Museum one rainy afternoon; and this chance overheard remark quite suddenly decided him.

Never again. Never. If he was a bad father, then he was bloody well going to *be* a bad father, and Amelia could learn to put up with it. It was a fact of her environment, and the sooner she learned to adapt to it the better. Learning to adapt to his environment has surely been one of the great survival mechanisms of Homo sapiens; and Amelia could damn well learn to survive that way too. She was a member of the goddam species, wasn't she? Well, then.

And so this, he resolved, was the finish. *Next* Sunday, he was going to stay in the flat and get on with his work; put in a real full day on it, as he'd been longing to do for weeks. And as for Amelia, she could like it or lump it. It wasn't as if she ever enjoyed herself anyway. No matter what he did with her, she was always bored, and so she might just as well be bored in the flat as anywhere else. Henceforth, he was no longer going to put himself out in the least degree for her entertainment.

And it was on the very next Sunday—the inaugural Sunday of this new and totally selfish regime—that the miracle came into being.

CHAPTER III

I T W A S T H I S miracle which now, four years later, he was
trying to explain to Rita down the telephone, but already he knew
it was hopeless. He could tell that it was by the very sound of her
breathing, even before she spoke.

"Hardly a *miracle!*" she commented, with a mocking little laugh;
and he wished, violently, that he's never told her anything about
it at all. "I mean," she went on, with that lilt of affectionate
raillery in her voice which had once so much excited him, but
which now—particularly down the telephone—merely sounded
shrill and patronising. "I mean, darling, there's nothing exactly
miraculous, is there, about a little girl going through a phase of
Daddy-worship? How old was she at that time? Nine, wasn't it?
That's just the age! The father-daughter thing, it's terribly well
known. It's in all the textbooks. You know, the Oedipus thing in
reverse, or do I mean Electra? Oh well, anyway, you know what
I mean."

Adrian knew what she meant all right. She meant that she had
felt rebuffed and hurt by his suggestion that she shouldn't return
to the flat till Monday; and had been hurt even more by his ill-
judged attempt at explanation. He had been a fool, he realised
now, to try to explain to Rita how much his daughter's weekly
visits meant to him. He couldn't expect her to understand, or to
feel other than jealous. Already, he sensed her hostility, before
she'd even met the girl.

"Daddy-worship"; "the Oedipus thing". Phrases like these, under
their guise of casual sophistication, were calculated to smear and
belittle. Their effect on a living, actual relationship was like selec-
tive weed-killer, attacking insidiously the sturdy, unselfconscious
roots of it.

Not that Rita would have thought all this out before slinging
this half-digested psychological jargon at him. She worked by
instinct, Rita did, and her instincts were always one jump ahead
of him. On whatever ground he tried to base an argument, he
would find that these grounds had already been mined beforehand.

The present case was typical. He'd tried to explain to her how he felt about these visits of Amelia's, which had been going on so happily and rewardingly for nearly four years now, and she didn't wait to understand, she didn't need to. At the first mention of the child's name, she had made a grab for the nearest cliché, and was there waiting for him with it, before he'd even assembled the relevant data.

In a way, he couldn't blame Rita for her resentment, or even for her mockery. The thing *did* sound soppy when it was put into words. But the whole beauty of it, with him and Amelia, was that they never *did* put it into words, had never had to. Even at the beginning—particularly, perhaps, at the beginning—it had been the very wordlessness of what was happening between them which had made it all so wonderful.

It hadn't happened all at once. In fact, in the very beginning, on that first Sunday of his revolt against the weekly outings which he found so irksome, he'd felt nothing but an uneasy guilt about what he was doing. Poor little girl! Expecting to be taken out somewhere, and then finding herself condemned to spend an entire afternoon cooped up in the company of a silent, preoccupied father who had no attention to spare for anything but the charts and diagrams spread in front of him on the forbidding great desk. He'd had the decency to warn her, of course. "I'm going to be busy," he'd told her the previous week, "I shan't be able to take you out anywhere next Sunday." And, "Yes, Daddy," she'd said, as she always did, her blue-green eyes fixed on him, and he didn't know whether she was listening or not. He never did.

He apologised again when the time came.

"'Im afraid it's going to be rather boring for you, chicken," he said, "I've got all this checking up to do, you see, and so you'll just . . . well, you'll just have to . . ."

He wished, at that point, that he'd laid in some toys, jigsaw puzzles or something, to put in front of her, like a saucer of milk in front of a cat, but he'd never thought about it.

"You'll just have to amuse yourself," he finished firmly, reminding himself again of Homo sapiens and all that; and, "Yes, Daddy," she said again. He turned away from her and bent over his work; and from then on he heard nothing from her for an hour.

For two hours. For three hours. It was only the necessity for turning the light on at a quarter past five that reminded him once

22

more of her existence. Turning in his revolving chair, and stretching his cramped spine, Adrian experienced quite a little shock at the sight of the two straggly plaits dangling barely eighteen inches from his knees. Amelia was lying full-length on the carpet, propped on her elbows, chin in hands, poring over the M–P volume of the *Encyclopaedia Britannica.*

He stared down at her. She was a good little thing, she really was! Not a sound out of her the whole afternoon.

"Tea, chicken?" he asked, with a twinge of belated compunction, and she looked up in a dazed, almost startled sort of a way. Then she smiled.

"What is there?" she asked; and after two or three more similarly laconic exchanges, the two of them were once more engrossed in their respective studies, she nibbling chocolate biscuits as she read, and he sipping a cup of Lapsang tea, pausing every now and then to check one of the digits on his chart against the notes that lay alongside.

It was seven o'clock before either of them spoke again.

"Did you know, Daddy, that Numitianus started a whole new *religion?*" remarked Amelia, as he helped her into her coat preparatory to taking her home, "An actual *religion,* called Numitianianism. And now nobody's even heard of it any more! Isn't that sad for him?"

Adrian suggested that since this Numitianus was dead and buried more than a thousand years, it couldn't matter to him whether his pet religion had caught on or not; but Amelia couldn't agree. They talked about it, on and off, all the way back in the car, and though the argument petered out quite inconclusively, Adrian went home with a strange and unfamiliar sense of accomplishment; a feeling of achievement for which he could find no adequate explanation. She really *is* a good little kid, was the nearest he could get to it: I really must try and ... oh, I don't know ... well ... something.

But by the next Sunday, he really *was* involved in a rush job, and so whatever resolutions he had made about entertaining Amelia more adequately had to go by the board. All afternoon long he worked on his report, and when, every now and again, he found a moment to glance at the child, there she was, just as she had been last week, stretched out on the carpet with her nose in a book. Only this time it wasn't the *Encyclopaedia Britannica,* it was Sir Robert

Ball's *Story of the Heavens*; and while they had tea—fish paste this time, on Matzo biscuits—she regaled Adrian with an account of the perturbations in the orbit of Uranus, and how they had led to the discovery of Neptune. Her voice grew shrill with mounting excitement as she approached the climactic moment when Le Verrier turned his telescope towards the area of the sky where he had calculated that Neptune should be—and there *was* Neptune!

As he listened, Adrian was aware, once again, of something happening which was outside the range of his previous experience, and for which he could find no words.

It was several Sundays later before he realised what it was.

Amelia loved him. She loved coming here, being with him. She loved the peace, the silence, the sense of intellectual purpose in this quiet, book-lined room. She loved the way he left her alone, the way he had his own work to do, and the fact that it was more important than she was, just as Neptune's orbit was more important than either of them.

They were two of a kind, he and Amelia. The struggle to be a "good father" was at an end. Amelia didn't need a "good father", had never needed one, she needed *him*.

"Adrian? . . . Are you still there? . . . I thought you must have hung up on me!"

Rita's voice, in spite of the little laugh, sounded anxious and accusatory. Adrian held the instrument a little away from his ear. The few inches of extra distance didn't really solve anything, any more than burning the electricity bill sets one's finances straight, but it did make him feel a little more in command of the situation, a little less like a puppet dancing to Rita's insistent tune. He wished he didn't know so exactly how she was feeling, there was nothing he could do about it, and it was both painful and boring to know it all so well. He knew exactly how she would be looking, over there in Wimbledon, sitting sideways to the telephone table, leaning forward from the waist, the lovely legs crossed, the tight, sullen little frown already puckering her white brow. Her pale, well-manicured fingers with their freshly-applied pink nail-varnish would by now be moving restlessly, like the quivering of poplar leaves before a storm, fidgeting with the receiver, plucking at the coiled snake of the flex. The small, neat lips would be delicately parted, poised for the attack, ready to snatch up the argument from wherever it might fall and worry it like a bone.

"I'd have *thought*," she was saying, stabbing at the words as was her habit when aggrieved, "I'd have *thought* that you'd be *pleased* that I'm so anxious to meet your Amelia! I don't *understand* you, Adrian! Don't you *want* us to meet...? To be friends...?"

Adrian was silent. He *didn't* want them to meet, and some dark instinct had already told him that they would never be friends. But of course, he couldn't say this. He wasn't happy even thinking it, it was so prejudiced, so irrational. How could he possibly know, in advance, whether Rita and Amelia were or weren't going to hit it off?

He just did know, that's all. He played for time.

"Look, darling," he said, "don't let's rush things. We don't want to spoil everything by—well—you know—just when Derek is beginning to come round and everything. . . ."

The sheer *non sequitur* of these considerations nearly stopped him in his tracks; but he knew he must keep going, keep talking, paper over the rift widening between them.

"So come as early as you possibly can, darling, on *Monday*," he urged, trying to put eager anticipation into his voice. "Come straight from work. Or if you like, we'll go out to dinner. I'll meet you at the . . ."

But she was not appeased.

"You're trying to put me off!" she accused, and he heard, with horror, the beginnings of tears in her voice. He could not bear it when she cried. "You don't *love* me any more! You don't *want* me to leave Derek and come to you, I can tell you don't . . ."

This was so nearly the truth that Adrian could not think what to say. In panic and confusion, he fell back on the old, despairing clichés.

Of course he still loved her. Of course he wanted her to come to him. But not yet. It was all so sudden . . .

"*Sudden!*" Rita fairly spat the word back at him, and who could blame her. "It's nearly four years since you first asked me to marry you! I was twenty-nine then, and now I'm thirty-three! Four bloody years of waiting, and working on Derek, and being faithful to you—do you realise I haven't let Derek make love to me *once*, in all that time . . .?"

He did know, but only because she'd told him so, repeatedly, over the years, always wanting from him some reaction of over-powering gratitude which he just couldn't dredge up. Such confidences embarrassed rather than flattered him, he didn't *want* to know about her and Derek, one way or the other. He wanted her marriage to be her problem, nothing to do with him, he didn't want the responsibility of it. The implicit demand that he should be spiritually in attendance in the Wimbledon bedroom, keeping Derek's hands off her, night after night, wearied him and made him feel uncomfortable.

But of course, there was no way of explaining this. He closed his eyes, and from six inches away let her indignation flow over and past him. At this distance from his ear, her voice sounded tinny and robot-like, spending its force on the electronic convolutions of the telephone service between here and Wimbledon.

"And what about *next* Sunday? And the Sunday after *that* ... and the Sunday after *that* ...?" Her distant anger was coming closer, and nothing could blot out the tears in her voice now. "... *all* the Sundays? We're planning to live together, that's what you said! So is *this* what it's going to be *like*? I'm to be thrown out *every* Sunday for the rest of my *life*? Thrown out of my own *home*, to walk the *streets* ...?"

"Darling, you're getting yourself worked up over nothing," he intervened, with exaggerated composure, knowing very well that it *wasn't* nothing, but not knowing how else to treat it. "We're not talking about *every* Sunday, we're talking about *next* Sunday! Give me a chance! It may not be sudden from *your*—I mean *our* point of view, but it's sudden for Amelia. Surely you can see that?"

She couldn't. She wouldn't. He'd had nearly *four years* to prepare Amelia for this outcome! Ever since she was nine years old, in fact—nearly a third of the kid's whole life, she was thirteen now, wasn't she? Surely, in all that time ...?

That a man could thus procrastinate, could put off a necessary but uncomfortable task week after week, month after month, for nearly four years, was beyond her comprehension. Or she claimed it was.

And why an *uncomfortable* task, anyway? Why not a delightful one? Why hadn't he presented the thing to Amelia as something exciting, something to look forward to? He could have played down the stepmother angle, after all Rita was a lot younger than he was, she would be more a sort of big sister to Amelia . . . a friend . . . someone to have fun with. The three of them could go on Sunday outings together. . . .

It was the word "outings" which caused the intake of breath through Adrian's teeth; but of course Rita couldn't have known that. She burst into tears.

"I don't know what to *do*!" she sobbed, collapsing at last into the simple, humiliating truth, all her defences down. "I told Derek *Sunday*," she wailed. "I *told* him I was leaving him *properly* on *Sunday*! *Now* what am I going to say?"

Adrian was sorry for her. This was something he remembered all too well from his own experience of a broken marriage: this desperate struggle to keep one's end up in the eyes of one's injured spouse, who, from the moment he or she learns of the Great Love, is going to be right there watching, sharp as a needle, for cracks to appear in it. He understood exactly the sort of humiliation it was going to be for Rita to have to go shamefacedly back to her husband with the news that actually Lover-boy didn't want her until Monday.

It was awful for her. He was truly sorry, and if she hadn't been in Wimbledon, he'd have put his arms round her and told her so.

But all the same, he wasn't going to give in. He had one last, desperate card to play, and he played it.

"I'll have to make sure that Dorothy doesn't mind," he said. "After all, she *is* the landlady. It's her house—" and he dropped the receiver into the cradle before Rita's entirely justified protests could rattle about his ears.

Because, of course, the objection was ludicrous. Dorothy never minded anything. A spinster in her late sixties, she had spent most of her adult life deliberately cultivating broad-mindedness as a substitute for everything that she might be thought to have missed out on in life; and so the idea that she might object to one of her tenants bringing his mistress to live with him was just simply laughable, and Rita knew this quite as well as he did.

It wouldn't make her laugh, though. That was the trouble.

CHAPTER IV

"SHE'S RATHER LIKE Anne Boleyn, *I* thought," said
Amelia, spooning sugar into the mug of strong tea which Dorothy,
all agog with curiosity, had set in front of her. "You know—black
almond-shaped eyes—well, almost black—and that very white skin.
The Spaniards remarked on how very white her skin was—Anne
Boleyn's, I mean—in one of their Despatches. And they said she
had six fingers, too, which was supposed to be a sign of witchcraft.
I looked to see if *She* has got six fingers, but she hasn't...."

Amelia pushed a strand of stringy, lightish hair out of the way
of her tea and drank thirstily, her pale rather small face almost lost
behind the huge mug. Dorothy, on the other side of the scrubbed
wooden table which was the central feature of her basement
kitchen, watched her young visitor with satisfaction. She always
liked it when Amelia came wandering down here for some part of
her Sunday afternoon visit to her father; and today there was the
additional excitement of being in on the girl's very first reactions
to the glamorous new arrival in her father's life. After four years
of having him all to herself, Sunday after Sunday, it was going to
be hard on the poor kiddie, she was sure to be jealous and miserable
about it, for a start, anyway. Unless, of course, Dorothy mused, it
didn't really make all that much difference to her? It wasn't as if
Mr Summers was the sort of father who'd ever put himself out
much for the child, or tried to amuse her; not as far back as
Dorothy could recall, anyway.

Not that Dorothy herself was all that concerned about amusing
Amelia either; it was more a question of Amelia amusing her. Now
that the girl was thirteen or so, she was beginning to be really good
company. There she would sit, chattering away, dropping an
innocent remark here or an unconscious hint there, from which
Dorothy was gradually enabled to build up, bit by bit, some sort of
a picture of life in that top flat where, for nearly four years now,
Adrian Summers had been keeping himself to himself with almost
impenetrable success.

He was a good tenant; she knew that much, of course. Right

from the start, she had had no doubts at all about taking him on. From her long years of experience as a landlady, she had summed him up instantly as a steady, responsible sort of a man, and it was plain that he had a decent job. Something to do with petroleum, he'd told her—Research Director in the Something-or-other Department. It sounded quite classy, anyway.

And her early judgement had been amply vindicated. Over the years, Mr Summers had proved himself quiet, reliable, and no trouble at all. An ideal tenant, really. The only trouble was that Dorothy, like so many landladies, didn't, in her heart of hearts, really like ideal tenants. They were no fun. They added no colour to existence. They were like guests at the bottle-party of life who hadn't brought a bottle with them.

Of course (as Dorothy would have been the first to admit) no sane landlady deliberately sets out to acquire tenants who are going to throw chairs at each other in the small hours or lock themselves in the bathroom screaming—and indeed, it would be difficult to frame an interview that would reliably select for this sort of thing—but all the same, if such things *should* chance to happen, there is no point in not making the best of them. And the best can sometimes be very, very good indeed.

And in a way, of course, she was being unfair. Her top-floor tenant was not what all landladies would have described as ideal, and he *did* have a private life of sorts going on up there, with his mistress slipping along Thursday afternoons as regular as clockwork, and often Tuesday evenings as well. But let's face it, it had been going on for years now, all the news-value had gone out of it. You couldn't shock the neighbours with something that went on and on like that, same time every week, and the same girl, too.

And so Amelia's revelation this afternoon that this Rita Langley was actually coming to *live* with Daddy had filled Dorothy with delightful anticipation. Him such a bookworm of a gentleman, and conceited with it, and her a common-or-garden minx—my goodness, now the sparks were going to fly!

She probed the child skilfully.

"Well, any time, dear, if you don't fancy being up there with the pair of them, you can always come down to old Dorothy. You know that, don't you? I'm always pleased to see you. And I wouldn't be surprised if I wouldn't be cooking gingerbread most Sundays from now on, or perhaps a date-loaf—remember you were asking me only the other day how to make those date-loaves of mine? Anyway, you'll be welcome any time you like to pop down. Because let's face it, it won't be quite the same now, will it, dear, for you and your Dad? Not with a third person, I mean. Two's company, they do say. . . ."

Amelia drew an end of wispy hair into her mouth to chew, and then almost spat it out, remembering. Mummy had threatened her with plaits again, like a baby, if she kept sucking the ends of her hair; but it wasn't this that was moving her to try and break herself of the habit. She knew well enough that Mummy would never stick to it, mothers never did, for the simple reason that the daughters always cared so much more, a million times more, about whatever was the thing that was being argued about, no mother could possibly stand up to it.

No, it wasn't Mummy's half-hearted threats that motivated her; it was something quite, quite different; something so new, so wonderful, that Amelia could as yet give no name to it, even in her own heart.

Mr Owen had arrived at the school only this term. He was the new English teacher, replacement for Miss Barbour, who had gone off to be a headmistress somewhere or other, and at first Amelia had hated and resented the change. Miss Barbour had been super, she'd read Kubla Khan as no one else in the world would ever read it; Amelia had listened spell-bound, hating from the bottom of her heart those girls who had giggled at the line:

As if this earth in fast thick pants were breathing. . . .

She could have killed them for making mock of so beautiful a poem read in so musical a voice.

And now this stout, bossy man with the horn-rimmed glasses and the North Country accent was having the impertinence to read to the class the very same poem! It was sacrilege! It was an insult to Miss Barbour's memory! *This* time, thought Amelia darkly, she, too, was going to giggle at the "Fast thick pants"!—*that* would show him where he got off! But no; perhaps, on second thoughts, it would be more dignified just not to listen at all, that would put him in his place better than anything!

The strong, resonant voice with the unfamiliar enlongated vowels boomed round the classroom, and Amelia put her fingers in her ears, hoping he would notice.

But he didn't. He wasn't looking at her at all, or at any of them, his eyes were fixed on his copy of *Selections from the Poets*:

> . . . Through caverrrns measoorless to maan
> Doon to a soon-less sea . . .

The feeble pressure of Amelia's fingers could do nothing against such resonance; she had no option but to listen, and by the time he had reached the final lines:

> Weave a saircle roond him twice
> And close your eyes with hooly dread,
> For he on hooney-dew hath fed
> And droonk the milk of Paradise.

By this time, she, too, had drunk the milk of Paradise.

She was in love.

Which was why it was now so important, so desperately and urgently important, to get out of this habit of sucking her hair. People who have drunk the milk of Paradise just *don't* bite the ends of their hair, and the thought that Mr Owen might one day actually catch her at it, might get a glimpse of the wet sticky spikes dangling against her blouse, making disgusting marks on it, filled her with horror.

"What" she said to Dorothy; and Dorothy good-humouredly repeated the gist of her remarks, ending up, this time, with the exhortation to Amelia, "Not to let them put your nose out of joint, dear!"

Daddy, too, had expected her to be jealous of Rita. Amelia felt embarrassed, and a little shocked at herself, for not feeling any of this expected resentment.

But the truth of the matter was that, for Amelia, curiosity had been overwhelmingly the most powerful emotion roused in her by her father's evasive and circumlocutory disclosures last week. Curiosity, and the exciting prospect of its imminent satisfaction, had effectively wiped out other possible discontents, and Amelia had looked forward to the coming Sunday with avidity. For years now she had been curious to learn more of this elusive, invisible woman whom everyone was so careful never to mention in her presence; and now, at last, the mystery was to be unveiled. She was actually to *see* the wicked, glittering creature; to talk with her, and see how Daddy behaved towards her.

"I'm going to have a *stepmother*!" she'd rather rashly—not to say prematurely—announced to a circle of awestruck classmates in the school playground. "A *step*mother! Isn't it *awful*!"—and having thus gathered around her an open-mouthed and admiring audience, agog for further details, it was rather a come-down to have to admit that she didn't even know if the lady in question was dark or fair; and that no, she couldn't say whether her father kissed her—you know—*properly*—or not, because she'd never actually seen them together....

All this was now to be remedied; and what with this, and with being in love with Mr Owen, and the whole world being so wonderful, jealousy didn't really come into it. Daddy's surprise and gratitude at her "taking it so well" made her feel rather mean for a moment, but there was no way of explaining her real feelings because they'd sound as if she didn't love Daddy as much as she used to do, and didn't care about their Sunday afternoons together any more.

Which wasn't the truth at all. She *did* enjoy coming here still, but of course it wasn't quite like it had been when she was a *little* girl. Then, Daddy's shadowy book-lined room, lit by the orangy glow of the standard lamp, had seemed like an Aladdin's cave of learning, infinite in its possibilities.

But now, at thirteen, she was becoming aware of the limitations of things. She had discovered that some of Daddy's books were boring; others incomprehensibly difficult. Of the ones she loved, many had become over-familiar through constant re-reading; and in any case, she often had homework to do now, and could no longer spend whole afternoons just browsing around the shelves at random. And there was another thing, too; when she *did* have a stretch of time to spare, she seemed, these days, to prefer writing to reading.

Particularly since the arrival in the universe of Mr Owen. Ever since the second week of term, she'd been secretly keeping a diary in which she recorded faithfully every glance he happened to throw in her direction, every word he ever addressed to her, even if it was only, "That'll do, Amelia," when she'd read on beyond her allotted portion of *Paradise Lost*.

She'd been lying on the floor bringing this slightly non-earth-

32

shaking narrative up to date this very afternoon, when Rita had suddenly turned up—and at this point in her reflections, Amelia remembered, with a little jolt of dismay, that in the excitement of the new arrival she'd forgotten to hide the precious volume away again! It must still be lying there, on the carpet, for all the world to see!

She jumped up, scraping her chair back from the table.

"Oh, Dorothy, may I bring my—well, a piece of work I'm doing —may I bring it down here to finish?" she asked urgently; and Dorothy nodded her head, and smiled to herself, knowingly.

Trouble already! It wasn't, naturally, that she *wanted* things to go wrong for Amelia—she was truly fond of the child. But all the same, if there *was* going to be trouble up in that top flat, then she, Dorothy, might just as well have a ringside seat for it.

It wasn't as if you made disasters *worse* by enjoying them; otherwise, every time there was a drought, all those sunbathers spread-eagled on beaches all over the world would have shrivelled the earth to a cinder by now, and brought all life to an end.

And they hadn't. So why pick on Dorothy?

Amelia hurried up the long flights of stairs anxiously. The diary didn't *look* like a diary, it looked like an ordinary school exercise book, with a red marbled cover. Certainly, *Daddy* would never think of looking at it, it would no more occur to him to wonder what his daughter had been writing, page after page, all through the long afternoon, than it would occur to *her* to check on his graphs and formulae.

But Rita was another matter. Rita was an unknown quantity, and might do *anything*.

The two of them drew apart, hastily, when Amelia burst into the room. Averting her eyes, she gathered up her property with all speed, and retreated. They *had* been kissing "properly", she felt sure, and so tomorrow she would be able to enlighten her playground audience, without, of course, letting on that she hadn't actually *seen* the phenomenon with her own eyes. Meanwhile, the diary was safe. It had been on the floor still, exactly where she had left it, and she felt sure that neither of the lovers had given it a glance.

"Keeping a diary, eh?" enquired Dorothy, her pale, allegedly short-sighted eyes behind their gold-rimmed spectacles taking in absolutely everything, as usual. "That's what my grandma used to do, keep a diary, when she was your age. I've still got it somewhere, quite an heirloom it is by now. *Her* name was Amelia, too. Funny!"

"Who? Your *grandmother*?" Amelia looked across the table at the lined, yellowish face, the sparse grey hair, and her mind lurched over the unimaginable vista of years and of events that had gone into the making of this moment, here, in this kitchen.... "Your *grandmother*? When she was a girl? Why, that would be—" she hesitated, not wanting to be rude "—that would be—well—almost Victorian times, wouldn't it?"

"Victorian times? Oh, my dear, oh, bless you, yes! Way back in ... now, let me see? My father was forty-one when ... and so that brings us to ... yes! It would have been back in the eighteen-fifties when my grandmother was growing up. Fifties and early sixties. ..."

Fifties and early sixties. The Fall of Sebastopol. The Charge of the Light Brigade. The shocking and blasphemous theories of Mr Charles Darwin, which the long-ago Amelia probably hadn't been allowed even to mention! What had it felt like to be alive when all this was happening, was news, not history yet at all?

"You mean you've still *got* it—your grandmother's diary? Oh, Dorothy, I'd *love* to see it—that is, if I may ... if you'd let me!" Amelia burst out. "We're doing the Factory Acts, you know, this term, and Lord Shaftesbury. I'd just love to know whether a little girl hearing about it at the time would have thought ..."

But Dorothy was hardly listening. Her eyes behind the thick lenses were shining, they had an almost greedy look, and Amelia realised that her request, far from seeming an impertinence, had for some reason been exactly what her companion had been waiting for. Had she even led the conversation in this direction deliberately, for some devious purpose of her own? Dorothy could be very devious, Amelia knew; but her motives were rarely hard to unravel if you just let her go on talking.

The present occasion was no exception.

"Amelia *Ponsonby*! That was her name!" she announced, with all the panache of a conjuror pulling the rabbit out of a hat; and when the present-day Amelia did not immediately react, she continued with undaunted showmanship (as the conjuror likewise has to when the children, who don't know where rabbits live anyway, accept with whey-faced unsurprise the fact that they live in hats): "One of *the* Ponsonbys, you know: cousins to Lord Dacre. . . ."— and then, lest anyone might accuse her of name-dropping, she hastily turned the thing into a bit of a joke:

"*Ha*ristocracy, that's me!" She patted her aproned bosom, and tittered a little. "True-blue *Har*ristocracy! What d'you think of that? Married beneath her, my grandma did, and what with that, and my father being the kind of gentleman he was, always in debt, that kind of thing, well, by the time I came along he hadn't a penny to bless himself with, and my mother had to take in Dressmaking and Alterations, and I went to the Board School like all the rest of the kids. Once in a while my father would find himself a job, but couldn't seem to hold anything down. He finished up on the dole, queueing up at the Labour Exchange with the rest of them.

"There was always something about him, though, my father, I remember him saying to me once, when he was quite an old man, 'Dorothy,' he said, 'don't ever forget who you are! It makes all the difference,' he told me, 'when they come to cut off the electricity, to know that you've got good blood in your veins. *Really* good blood. It kind of gives you the upper hand of them, while you sit there in the dark, and can't even make a cup of tea.' And in a way, you know, I could see what he meant, though I did wish, sometimes, that he could have kept off the gambling instead. That was what killed my poor mother in the end. . . ."

Amelia wriggled a little, and tried to decide if it would be rude to interrupt. She'd heard many times about Dorothy's mother and the gambling debts and how they went to her lungs, poor soul. It was quite an interesting story, and Dorothy told it with an impassioned sense of the injustice of things which gave it all the flavour of a moral tale—though the moral, it must be admitted, was a confused one, to the effect (so far as Amelia could make out) that gambling is the most aristocratic of all the deadly sins; once a gentleman always a gentleman; and that dying wives shouldn't scream about money out of the bedroom window, it lowers the tone.

"The diary?" prompted Amelia, as soon as it seemed at all polite to do so; and Dorothy's hand flew to her brow, in an elaborate pantomime of having forgotten all about it.

Was Amelia sure she wanted to see it? Wouldn't she get fed up with all those dead and gone people with all those long strings of

35

names they used to go in for—The Lady Patricia Tyssen-Tucke who used to be such a regular visitor? The Honourable Mrs Moreton-Parkes, sister-in-law to the Duke of Connaught...? All the while she was protesting, Dorothy was edging her way to the door, past the big table, past the rocking-chair and the old-fashioned dresser.

"I'll be right back—you stay where you are," she ordered, and, wiping her hands purposefully on her apron, she hurried out of the kitchen, her cumbersome backside quite wobbling with the urgency of it.

She returned several minutes later with a stout leather volume with gilt clasps under one arm, and on the other ...

"Oh *no*, Dorothy!" Amelia cried, half-laughing. "Not again...!"

A little sheepishly, Dorothy glanced down sidelong at the heavy, red-faced baby in the crook of her arm. She clicked her tongue at it, joggled it absently, then looked up to face Amelia.

"Well, I know, dear, but what can you do? Brian's back, you see, I heard Kathy crying as I came past their door, so I just peeked in, and there he was, sprawled out across the bed, rucksack and all, and his boots still on! The nerve of him! And after all these weeks without so much as a postcard, and poor Kath fit to break her heart over him! Still, it's none of *my* business. She's over the moon now, of course, she can't stop crying, and I could see right away that Baby was never going to get any supper, not at that rate, he was yelling his head off, poor little mite, and neither of them taking a blind bit of notice! So I told Kathy, I said if she wanted I'd make up his bottle down here, just this once, so she can give her mind to the one thing at a time. Of course, I could see how it was: I reckon she's scared that if she knocks off to feed the baby, that fellow of hers'll be off again. You know how it is."

Amelia didn't know, but was always ready to learn. With a certain distaste (because he looked damp) she allowed Dorothy to plump the baby in her lap, and then sat, clutching him inexpertly, while Dorothy busied herself at the cooker preparing the bottle.

"You know, Dorothy," she ventured after a minute or two, "you're much too kind to everybody, you really are! All this baby-sitting for Kathy and Brian—they shouldn't expect you to do it, it's not fair. He's *their* baby. They had him because they believed in freedom, and the Life Force, and the pulse of the universe, and all that sort of thing; but they never asked *you* what *you* believed in, did they? So why should *you* always be the one to give him his bottle?"

Dorothy shook her head. Amelia's logical mind always impressed her, but when a baby is hungry and his mother crying, and the chap with the rucksack mightn't even *be* the father if all were known—well, in such a case warm milk seemed to Dorothy to be the obvious answer. She fitted the teat on to the bottle and reclaimed the baby from Amelia. No good offering to let her feed him, she was obviously ill at ease with the little creature. She just wasn't a motherly sort of child, never had been. Dorothy could never remember her playing with dolls even when she was quite a little thing, when Mr Summers had first come to live here.

And he *was* wet, it was quite true. Dorothy spread a folded towel over her black woollen skirt, and settling down with baby and bottle, her plump knees spread wide, she proceeded to give Amelia a brief run-through of her own theories about what was going on up there on the first floor, including a short but colourful resumé of what she, Dorothy, would tell that useless, big-headed oaf if *she* was in Kathy's position.

But there, what was the good of talking? "These young girls, they seem to have no fight in them, not like *we* used to have. I suppose it's all these Health Foods they eat, wheat-germ and that."

By the time her conversation with Dorothy was over, and she had returned upstairs, it was the hour—indeed past the hour—for Amelia to set off home. Her father stood, swinging the car-keys by one finger, while she rushed around the flat collecting her belongings and putting on her coat and scarf. Only at the last moment did Rita emerge from the bedroom to bid her good-bye, which she did in tones of such silky sweetness that Amelia felt stupid and awkward, and could not think how to reply.

"G'bye," she muttered to the floor at Rita's feet; and during the drive home she wondered, for the first time in years, whether her father's silence meant that he was cross with her? Usually, their silences were such companionable ones, betokening nothing more than the fact that they both felt more like thinking than talking; but this one was different, somehow.

CHAPTER V

MOTHERS OF COURSE, aren't as easy to talk to as
landladies. They are too frightened. Amelia had yet to learn that
the only really satisfactory confidante for your troubles is someone
who enjoys them, and this inevitably cuts out anyone who actually
loves you. Particularly does it cut out your mother, who loves you
very much indeed and therefore cannot possibly enjoy your troubles.
She hates them, she is terrified of them, you'd have to be a sadist
deliberately to impose them on her.

Which is a pity, because of course mothers understand the way
you are feeling better than anyone, they are bound to, they have so
much more data to go on. Even quite stupid mothers, Amelia reflected (and Mummy wasn't stupid at all), even stupid mothers have
at their finger-tips more data about you than anyone else in the
whole world. They have watched you eating, sleeping, sulking,
laughing, being sick, showing off to visitors. They know every single
kind of food you like and don't like, and they know from your very
footstep on the stairs whether you are going to do your practising
properly or not. They have no letters after their names, but in their
narrow and highly-specialised field—*you*—they are world experts,
there is not a psychologist on earth who can touch them. A psychologist has had, at most, a seven-year training, comprising a variety
of topics; and what is this in comparison with the thirteen years
of non-stop specialised training to which Peggy had subjected herself in bringing up Amelia? Sitting up with her all night when she
had croup; inventing a kind of rounders that could be played even
with a sprained ankle; turning a painful visit to the dentist into an
enchantment by sketching in the margin of *Country Life* caricatures
of all the glum faces ranged around the waiting-room, and giving
them titles like Lady Nose, and Madame Slippe-Showing, and
Lord Wype-Specs—until Amelia was reduced to such giggles as to
make the subsequent ordeal in the surgery something utterly trivial,
leaving practically no mark on her memory at all.

All this, and fires too. Blazing coal fires to come home to out of
the wintry dusk. Tea with dripping-toast, buns. . . sympathy about

the unfairness of the geography test. Pocket-money . . . Saturday shopping . . . summer frocks in new bright cotton rolling off Mummy's sewing-machine into the long vista of summer time. Picnics, swimming, and long drinks of Mummy's home-made lemonade, squeezed from real lemons, as you sat on the dry August lawn, the heat prickling your bottom through your thin summer pants.

Mummy. Provider of all this. Provider, too, of a kitten, a tiny orange kitten, curled up on Amelia's bed for a surprise, a few days after Daddy went away. A kitten that purred and purred, nuzzling its tiny pink nose against her giant forefinger in utter trust, as if it had known, all its tiny life long, that it was going to be Amelia's kitten, and no one else's.

"Esben" she called it, because of the story of "Esben and the Witch", in the *Pink Fairy Book*. Mummy re-read the story to her that same night, and Amelia had loved it, and the kitten, curled up on her lap, had loved it too.

> Fly quick, my little stick
> Carry me across the stream!

sang Esben in the story; and only now, four years later, did Amelia recall that Mummy had been nearly crying the whole time. Mummy had tried very hard not to cry, Amelia remembered, throughout those first weeks, and Amelia had tried as best she could to help her, putting her arms round her neck, and bringing her cups of tea in bed, all slopped in the saucer. For Amelia herself, this had been a fairly happy time, but only because Mummy, in the teeth of everything, had forced it to be so: like a skilled gardener forcing strawberries out of season with the aid of artificial heat and light.

> Fly quick, my little stick,
> Carry me across the stream!

—and across the stream they had been carried, Mummy guarding and watching over her every inch of the precarious way.

Mummy. Mummy, guardian of the years, the gravitational centre of all that happened. Mummy, who loved her as no one else would ever love her again—how was it—how *could* it be?—that it was to Mummy alone that Amelia could not tell the story of her afternoon with Daddy and the girlfriend?

She'd been able to tell it to *Dorothy* all right; tell her every

39

thrilling detail, from Rita's low-slung hairstyle to her pink, tapered finger-nails and her imitation-crocodile boots. Had told her, too (making them both laugh in the telling), how Rita had fidgeted about the room, pretending to be interested in Adrian's books, pulling out first one and then another from the shelves in a silly, vacant sort of way, not a bit as if she wanted to read them, but rather as if she was trying to annoy them, to punish them for being beyond her, and for keeping secrets from her within their quiet covers.

Mummy would have loved to hear all this, and would have laughed just as heartily as Dorothy did, and with a good deal more appreciation. She would have delighted, too, in Amelia's account of the phone-call to Poor Derek, all about a chocolate-covered Swiss roll which someone had brought to Wimbledon as a present to someone else, and would now be mortally offended if it wasn't taken round instantly (by Derek) to somewhere in Wood Green.

"But, Derek, if you don't take it today it'll get *stale*!" Rita kept howling; and then, "But that's not the same thing at *all*!" she shrieked, evidently in response to a suggestion of Derek's that for a quarter the price of his petrol, the Someone in Wood Green could buy their own chocolate-covered Swiss roll.

"*Men!*" Rita had exploded, slamming down the phone, and while Adrian continued to work on his report, she proceeded to explain the whole thing to him, including the price of chocolate-coated Swiss rolls at Tesco's as compared with Marks and Spencer.

"*You* wouldn't have let me down like that, would you, darling?" she finished, folding her arms round Adrian's neck from behind: and Adrian, his eyes still on his work, agreed absently and quite at random that No, of course he wouldn't.

"And I wish I could be there when he says '*What* chocolate-coated Swiss roll?'" Amelia would have finished her recital gaily; and Mummy would have loved it. They'd have laughed and laughed.

Why, *why*, then, was it so difficult? So impossible, even? And yet it had been so easy with Dorothy—with *anyone*, in fact, except Mummy. Anyone else at all. The girls at school, for instance, there'd be no difficulty at all about telling *them*—though of course in this case she'd select from her material on a rather different basis. With them, she'd be borne along on their expectations as on an incoming tide, telling them the things they wanted to hear, throwing in facts and oddments of truth when and as convenient, but not allowing such items to take over too much and spoil the total effect.

Yes, she would admit, with perhaps a little yawn, to show how blasé she was about the whole thing, yes, it *is* a bit of a responsibility being a stepdaughter. You know what stepmothers *are*, so inclined to be jealous and all that. The trouble is, you see, that they aren't real blood-relations to your father the way you are, and of course they feel it, poor things. I have to be terribly careful not to let Daddy be too nice to me while *she's* there. Gosh, you should have just seen the look on her face when he swung me up in his arms last time when I arrived...! I thought she'd have *killed* me...!

That would be the line at school—nonchalant, detached, and gently tolerant towards the problems of the poor tangled adults. Perhaps Mr Owen would be on playground duty, and would notice the little crowd gathering. "Why, it's Amelia Summers!" he would say to himself, strolling a little nearer, "What a very popular girl she appears to be ... I wonder what she is saying...?" And maybe he would stroll nearer still, catch snatches of her words. And then ... maybe. ...

"Nothing much," she heard herself saying sullenly in answer to one of her mother's eager queries about the afternoon: and, "Not very," was all she could think of to answer the anxious enquiry as to whether she'd thought Rita pretty.

Was she nice? Did you like her? Can she cook? Was it a nice tea? Has she a job?

Not very. Fairly. I don't know. More or less. I didn't ask her.

The sulky monosyllables filled Amelia herself with shame, and a great sadness, yet somehow there was nothing she could do about it. Not a word of real information could be she bring herself to divulge.

And it wasn't a question of loyalty, not to either parent. Since the divorce, Daddy had made no secret of Rita's association with him—if anything, he seemed rather to like the idea that people should know about it, as if it was a book he had published or something, whose success would be boosted by a bit of publicity.

And as for Mummy, she'd known about Rita for ages—right from the very beginning, in fact, and it was years since she'd cried over it or gone around looking miserable. There was no doubt at all that, by now, Mummy would enjoy a good gossip about Rita—her hair-style, her clothes, her table manners, her intellect, if any. Such a cosy, gossipy evening it could have been, with the drawing-room fire burning brightly, the copper bowl with the beech leaves in it dancing and flickering in the shadows like a second fire; and Esben giving the final touches to the scene by lying curled up on the hearthrug, a golden ball of satisfaction so absolute that it did not even need to purr. Such an evening it was for confidences, and laughter, and little, scandalous revelations.

"Look, Mummy, look, this is how she walks!" Amelia could have exclaimed, "Like this—sort of teetering backwards on to the heels of those dreadful boots...!"—and Mummy would have laughed delightedly while Amelia tottered ridiculously round the room. And under the spur of this audience response, Amelia's gift for mimicry would have gone from strength to strength:

"Listen, Mummy, this is how she says 'Da-a-ahling!' when she wants Daddy to do something for her! All sort of drawly and languishing—'da-a-ahling, I *do* wish you'd sometimes remember to...'"

How they'd have laughed, she and Mummy, in that lovely cosy intimacy, tearing Rita to pieces by the light of the glowing fire! How close they would have felt, how safe!

"*Mummy—!*"

But it was impossible. It just couldn't be done. Trying not to see the sudden flash of hope and eagerness in her mother's face, followed by the sagging of disappointment, Amelia gathered up her books and her cardigan and humped herself to her feet.

"Homework," she muttered, face averted, and trailed out of the door, flinging it open noisily and almost slamming it behind her with shame and remorse.

Upstairs in her own little room, with the pictures of prehistoric monsters on the walls, and the electric fire with the imitation coals which Mummy had tried to persuade her not to choose because it was vulgar, she began to feel better.

She hadn't really anything much to do. She had finished her homework at Daddy's, and had brought her diary up to date, too, though this had been a less tranquil activity than usual because of Rita being there, and fidgeting about the room all the time so that you never knew when she might be looking over your shoulder;

Amelia had kept having to cover the page with her elbow whenever Rita seemed to be moving in her direction, and this meant that the passages written up today were more disjointed than usual. Amelia opened the marbled covers of the exercise book, and, lying full-length on her bed, re-read the last few pages of what she had written this afternoon:

Wednesday, March 3rd
Mr O. was late this morning, he came into prayers just before the hymn, and he leaned over Daphne to see the place in her book. Over *Daphne!* Oh, God, why couldn't *I* have been at the end of a row this morning, then he'd have leaned over *me!* Oh, cruel Fate! And then, when we filed out, there was such a squash through the big doors I couldn't get through quick enough, and so all I saw was his back disappearing down the staff-room corridor!

What a wonderful way he walks, with such a swing to his movements, as if he owned the world.

He *does* own my world, little does he know!

Thursday, March 4th
No English lesson today! Doom, doom, doom! The day is a desert that I have to cross without food or water.

One tiny ray of light—I saw him going along the corridor while I stood in the dinner-queue, but he didn't see me.

Daphne says he's married. I didn't want her to think I was upset, so I just said, "Yes, I know." Well, I did know, didn't I, because she'd just told me, so it wasn't actually a lie.

They are *not* going to know that I mind. Not, not, not.

And I *don't* mind, I *DON'T*! I've been thinking about it all through chemistry, my nitrous oxide wouldn't support combustion at all, not for a second, I put taper after taper into it and they just went out. But of course I didn't put that in my notes because really I know it *does* support combustion, it says so in our book as well as Miss Harland.

My heart is no longer broken, him being married is nothing to me, mine is a higher kind of love, I just want him to exist in the Universe, and he *does* exist.

Daphne doesn't understand about love, I have to say it, even though she's my best friend.

Tomorrow we get back our essays!!!!

Friday, March 5th
Got our Milton essays back! He didn't read mine out, but he *did* write two lines at the end of it! Two whole lines! I shall cut them out and paste them in here so that they may be preserved for ever in his own handwriting:

> "Quite good, but *please*, not such long quotations. I do know the poem, you know!"

Just imagine, he must have been *smiling* while he wrote it! That little crooked, cynical smile that makes his eyebrows tilt, and he was smiling about *me*! About Amelia Summers! Me, me, me!
I'm so glad my name is Amelia, and not Jean or something.

This was the latest entry. Amelia read it through once more, and then, sleepy though she was by now, she decided to make a start on the leather-bound diary of Dorothy's grandmother. She had promised Dorothy that she would bring it back without fail on the following Sunday, and there mightn't be much time for it during the week. She had already ascertained, by a swift glance through, that it was quite long, and that the writing, though neat and carefully penned, was in an unfamiliar style and, as Dorothy had said, somewhat hard to read until you got used to it.

Slowly, she unfastened the gilt clasps and raised the leather cover. On the fly-leaf was written:

Amelia Caroline Ponsonby. Her Book.
Presented on this Day of her Fourteenth Birthday
February 12th, 1854
By her Loving Godmother, Henrietta Mary Mills.
"May she dwell in the Light of the Lord"

CHAPTER VI

"*What* CHOCOLATE-COATED Swiss roll?" asked Adrian, just as Amelia had predicted; and Rita, equally predictably, burst into tears.

It was a difficult quarrel to launch, because Adrian, just sitting down to his work after driving Amelia home, really *didn't* know what in the world Rita was talking about, had no recollection of the subject at all. And by the time she had explained it to him all over again, including the comparative prices of chocolate-coated Swiss rolls at Tesco's and at Marks and Spencer, he once more had on his face the glazed expression which had so incensed her in the first place.

"You *never* listen to me," she sobbed, "you never listen to a word I say!" and Adrian, knowing that he didn't, said, "Nonsense, darling," rather helplessly.

He was dismayed, and also puzzled by her outburst. It had seemed to him that the afternoon had gone off quite reasonably well, with Amelia down with Dorothy half the time, Rita chattering away, and he, Adrian, managing to get quite a fair amount of work done in spite of it all.

What had gone wrong? Whatever *was* she on about?

"Look, dear," he said, trying to be placatory, "if Amelia has upset you some way about a Swiss roll, then I'm sorry. She *can* be rather a little pig sometimes, I suppose. Though actually I thought she was behaving very well most of the time. I mean, she could hardly have been less bother, could she? First down at Dorothy's, and then just lying on the floor reading and getting on with her homework . . . she hardly spoke a word the entire afternoon."

"And *that's* what you call 'behaving well?' Is *that* the way you think a kid of thirteen ought to be? Let me tell you something, Adrian, if that child was *my* daughter, which thank heaven she's not, I'd be very, very worried about her. I would, Adrian. All that reading, and writing, and so quiet all the time, it's not natural. And so secretive, too, so sly—you've only got to stir out of your chair and she covers up what she's doing as if you were a spy, or something! What's she trying to hide? What is it she's so ashamed of? Morbid, I call it. At her age, she should be full of fun and chatter, she should be active, outgoing, communicative. I don't want to scare you, Adrian, but as her father, I think you should be doing something about it. Get some advice about her. There are clinics. . . ."

Adrian closed his eyes, crossed his legs, and leaned back in his chair.

"What you mean is, you're bored," he said to Rita. "Amelia and I both have work to do on Sundays, and you haven't. And so you feel left out. Of course you do. But I did tell you. I warned you right from the start that our Sundays are like this. I knew you wouldn't enjoy it, I knew it wasn't your thing, but you *would* come. . . ."

" '*Come*'? I like that!" Rita was outraged. "Adrian, I *live* here! Hadn't you noticed? Or are you telling me I'm to be chucked out of *my* own home every Sunday of my life for the sake of that little zombie? Why don't you think about chucking *her* out for a change? It'd do her good, she needs a bit of fresh air. She ought to be out and about with her friends at weekends, not humped over her books in a bad light, and breathing through her mouth half the time! She'll end up with short sight, adenoids, curvature of the spine. . . ."

Adrian once again closed his eyes, and laid down his pen with an air of exaggerated weariness.

"You can't 'end up' with short sight," he explained patiently. "It's a thing you're born with. It's genetic."

The word was a trigger word. Rita's brain was instantly ablaze with all the popular medical articles she'd skimmed through in magazines recently, and at once she plunged, with crusaders' zeal, into a passionate account of this survey or something that some Doctor Somebody had been conducting in America or somewhere, which showed that more children who wore glasses had learned to read early, or was it that they stopped wearing glasses when they stopped reading, or maybe the other way round, but anyway, what is proved conclusively was that short sight *wasn't* genetic, it was due to reading too much, and look at primitive man, *he* didn't read at all, and didn't need glasses either, so there!

Adrian sighed. His report would just have to be finished in his lunch-hour, that was all. It was going to be the same next week, too, and the week after.

He swivelled round in his chair and faced Rita. In a way, he was glad they were quarrelling, because it absolved him at least for the time being of any obligation to feel in love with her. Since she had moved in with him, and everything was suddenly supposed to be so marvellous, the tepid quality of his feelings towards her had terrified him. He had searched for the old passion with the desperation of a man searching for his passport in an airport departure lounge ... it *must* be here ... it *must* ... I *know* I had it. ...

But now, with Rita nagging and scolding like this, he had a sudden sense of reprieve. She wasn't even attractive, her white forehead all screwed up and her eyes bulging with temper ... he couldn't possibly love her like that, no one could. And since this was a quarrel, he didn't *have* to love her, in fact he could hate her if he liked, hatred is allowed during a quarrel. It's the love-hate thing, hatred the reverse side of love, and all that. He felt thankful that it *had* a reverse side, it gave you a sort of rest now and again. ...

And what's more, he didn't have to put up with her stupid, female illogic, either.

"Look," he said, "Amelia is *my* daughter, and so perhaps you'll be good enough to allow me to be the best judge? She happens to be an intelligent child, and she likes to have a bit of peace and quiet now and again to read and think. Just as I do. We're alike, Amelia and I. Hell, we *are* father and daughter. ..."

He stopped, realising that by this phrase he was laying himself open to yet another explosion of amateur psychology. He went on, in a slightly more conciliatory tone:

"And anyway, Rita, you must realise that Amelia's only two years off O levels now. She has homework to do."

"*Homework!*" Rita drawled the word with heavy, deliberate insolence. "You don't know you're born, Adrian, the way you let that child pull the wool over your eyes. That wasn't *homework* she was doing this afternoon, don't you believe it! What sort of 'homework' could it be that consists simply of scribbling page after page of huge, untidy writing, and never once having to stop to think, or to look anything up? Didn't you *notice* what a scrawl it was? What sort of a father *are* you? Don't you notice *anything*?"

47

"Notice? No, of course I don't notice. Why should I pry into what she's doing? She does her stuff, I do mine, it's been like that for four years now, and we're both perfectly happy with it. I'm sorry if you're bored, Rita, but it *is* only one afternoon in the week. Can't you do some sewing or something—?" and then, when Rita's head jerked up in fury, he hastily amended "well, whatever it is you do like doing. It isn't even a whole afternoon, usually. She's down with Dorothy part of the time...."

"Oh, big deal! And that's another thing, while we're on the subject. What sort of company do you think that old woman is for your precious little ewe-lamb? Have you any idea what they *talk* about when they're down there together? Of course you haven't! Up here in your ivory tower, you haven't the faintest inkling of what goes on! Well, I'll tell you one thing: if it was *my* daughter I'd see her dead and in her grave before I'd send her down there to have her mind poisoned by that filthy-minded eavesdropping old harridan...."

"Let me see, they were making gingerbread this time, weren't they?" Adrian remarked, as annoyingly as he knew how. "Amelia brought some up for tea, if you remember. It was rather good, I think you said..."

"*I* said? Why, I never even..."

"But of course," continued Adrian smoothly, "the witch in Hansel and Gretel was also very good at making gingerbread, was she not? Is that what you had in mind?"

Rita clenched and unclenched her white knuckles. She knew that Adrian was taking the mickey in his effortless, intellectualising way, but she couldn't grasp his meaning sufficiently to be ready with an appropriate come-back. So she did the only other thing she could do: she burst into tears.

The reconciliation was sweet, though perhaps a little perfunctory on Adrian's part, as he was anxious to get back to his work. He was relieved, and very pleasantly surprised, that Rita seemed unperturbed by the slightly unflattering haste with which he scrambled back into his clothes and reseated himself at the desk. She even had a little smile playing around her lips as she lay and watched him.

"*I'll show him!*" she was thinking. "Just let him wait! *I'll* teach him!"

48

CHAPTER VII

At the sight of the careful, faded handwriting of so long ago, Amelia's sleepiness left her, and with a little *frisson* of excitement she turned over the first of the fragile, whispering pages, and began to read:

February 13th, 1854
I, Amelia Caroline Ponsonby, aged 14 yrs and one day, am about to pen the first, momentous words of this my Journal.

Would that I could think of words worthy of so solemn an occasion, for it is in no light spirit that I lay my hand to this task. This Journal which I begin today will be with me all my life long. Thru' all the years to come, I shall confide to these pages all my Joys and my Sorrows, and even my Sins, and the most hidden Secrets of my Heart.

May the Good Lord keep me from Sins that are as Scarlet, and I pray that I may never need to confide any Such to this Journal. May no eyes other than mine ever look upon these pages, save only the Eye of God Almighty.

Mamma says that 2¾ yards of Petersham should be sufficient for the braiding of my dress, but Mrs T. declares she will need 3 at least, to allow for turnings.

There was something distinctly reassuring about this last sentence. If the hidden secrets of Miss Amelia Ponsonby's heart were to be of this calibre, then surely one need feel no guilt at perusing them?

Because a few moments earlier, the Amelia of the 1970s *had* been feeling guilty. All that about, "No other eyes than mine . . ." —well, it did make you think. The long-ago Amelia could hardly have made her wishes in the matter plainer, or more emphatic.

Still—a hundred *years*! More than a hundred! The childish hand which had formed that careful copperplate had been dust these many decades; the secrets of the childish heart were gone as if they had never been, like a candle-flame long blown out.

A hundred years! How would *I* feel, Amelia asked herself, if they were to find *my* diary after all that time, and read the things I've written about Mr Owen? About him leaning over Daphne's shoulder, and what she said afterwards? I'd *die*, of course, if anyone were to read it *now* : but after more than a hundred years. . . . ?

In a hundred years, Daphne, herself, and Mr Owen would all be dead and in their graves. At the thought of herself and Mr Owen (she couldn't be bothered about Daphne) being dead and in their graves, warm, delicious tears began to trickle down Amelia's cheeks, and she began composing epitaphs for their lonely moorland tomb:

> "Here lie two lovers, hearts entwined."
> "Even in Death were they not divided."
> "Amor vincit Omnia"

—as, indeed, it would need to do if the two of them were to fetch up in the same grave despite Mr Owen being a married man.

Brushing the tears from her eyes, Amelia turned another of the brittle pages, and read on:

February 18th
Our new governess arrived this morning. Jevons took the carriage to meet the Coach at Penton's Corner, and Thomas went with him to help with her boxes. I did so wish to go in the carriage with them, and be the very first to see Miss Overton, but Mamma said it would be most improper. Hester and I are to wait in the schoolroom, she says, until she brings Miss Overton up to be introduced.

Oh, dear, what a long, wearisome morning! Hester and I sat in the Oriel seat, watching from the schoolroom window, for more than an hour. When the carriage finally came into sight round the turn of the drive, and drew up outside the house, we were so excited we could hardly refrain from craning our necks to see her alighting, which would have been very ill-bred, and Mamma would have been most vexed.

February 19th
I think I like Miss Overton. She has pleasing blue eyes and a refined manner, and she says that my drawings are unusually good for my age, and most tastefully executed.

Hester, I am sorry to say, has made up her mind to dislike her.

She declares that she is not a lady, which is absurd, because Mamma would never allow us to be taught by a person who was not a lady. Besides, she came to us from Lady Rochford's household, so her social standing must, I am sure, be impeccable.

I think Hester is out of temper because Miss O. did not say anything about *her* drawings. Hester does not like having to be in the schoolroom still, now that she is nearly sixteen, but Mamma says she still has a lot to learn, and must go on having lessons with me for at least another year.

February 23rd
Hester still very out of temper. She was almost *rude* to Miss Overton on our walk this afternoon, and I threatened that I'd tell Mamma.

I would not have done so, naturally, but she is nevertheless being most unkind and unsisterly towards me this evening. She will not give me my music back, I cannot practice without it, and Mamma was very vexed with me. It is most unjust and unfair. . . .

And so on and so on. The modern Amelia began to skip bits here and there. It was quite interesting in a way, but what about History? What about the Crimean War? The Chartist riots? The publication of *In Memoriam*? This Amelia Ponsonby might just as well not have lived in History at all, for all the notice she took of it. While children in their thousands were starving to death in the streets, while the great cholera epidemic raged, and Sebastapol was falling, here was Miss Amelia Ponsonby lamenting her Mamma's refusal to allow her to have a dress made up in figured lilac satinet.

"I'm *not* too young for it," she raged in the pages of her Journal, "and if I am, then so is Hester, too! She's not 'out' yet, she's only in the schoolroom still, just as I am!"

Soldiers died. Politicians rose and crashed. Poor harvests plus economic bungling brought destitution to millions; and here is Amelia Caroline Ponsonby forbidden to wear figured lilac satinet.

And what about all those "hidden secrets of her heart"? Amelia skimmed through the pages . . . spring . . . summer . . . autumn . . . for her, they slipped by in seconds, but of course her namesake had had to live through them.

Ah, this was more like it!

November 3rd, 1854
... I knew, without looking round, that Mr B. was still there, and so I contrived to leave my prayer-book in the corner of the pew, and I didn't tell Papa about it till we were outside in the churchyard. He was vexed, but he allowed me to go back into the church for it while he waited.

Oh, Journal, my Journal, how can I express to you my joy! *He was still there!* He was stacking the hassocks at the end of each pew, and he *saw* me! He *spoke* to me!

'Have you lost something, Miss Ponsonby?' he asked me, and his voice, though very respectful, was somehow full of a wonderful power, and yet gentle, too. I don't know what I said, I could scarcely breathe, but I must have answered something, because a moment later he was handing me my prayer-book, with a little bow. He walked with me all the way to the church door, and then he stood there, watching, until he saw me rejoin Papa at the gate.

O, Posterity, Posterity, if ever you read these words, share with me in my great joy! I did not know there was such happiness in the whole world!

"Mr B." Amelia had a little trouble identifying this character, and had to turn back a number of pages before she discovered that he was the new curate, who had taken up his duties at the end of the summer. But from this point on, as page followed page, she never again had to seek out references to him: he featured in every single entry, though often in a sadly negative rôle:

Mr B. was not there
  Did not see Mr B. at all today. Tried to get Miss O. to come home past the new School building, but she said no, we would be late for tea, and it would vex Mamma.

This last entry ended with a little prayer:

O Lord God, who art merciful, I pray you put it into Miss O.'s head to come home from our afternoon walk past the School tomorrow. If you will just do this for me, O Lord, I will be thy meek and humble servant for ever. I will be full of forgiveness and loving-kindness towards all the creatures, even Hester.

Whether or not this prayer was answered must remain for ever in doubt, for there was no entry for the following day. Nor for the next ... nor the next. It was more than a week later before the tale was taken up again:

November 21st, 1854
I have it on good authority that tomorrow, at three o'clock in the afternoon, the Choir will be practicing the new anthem, with Mr B. in attendance! I will, I will, I *will* go with Aunt Sophie at that hour to put flowers on Grandmamma's grave! He is sure to come through the churchyard, and I will persuade Aunt Sophie to wait there a while, talking about dear Grandmamma, until he comes. . . .

November 22nd
I saw him! I saw him! He was talking to one of the choir boys as he came into the churchyard, but he saw us, I know he did, he came right up to us just as we were laying down the flowers. He stopped, and he said something to Aunt Sophie, and I am certain that he smiled at me, but I was too bashful to look up.

Oh, would that I were bolder! But maybe he does not like a girl to be bold? I would hate to be bold and displease him, so perhaps it was all for the best that I kept my eyes on the ground.

November 23rd
Aunt Sophie told Mamma I was a dear, good girl, remembering Grandmamma so lovingly, and so I am to go with her next week, too, when she takes the flowers.

Oh joy, oh joy!

Hester would say that these are wrong thoughts, to be taking flowers to poor Grandmamma's grave in such a spirit of rejoicing, and only in order to meet Mr B. at her graveside.

But I don't think they are. When *I* am a grandmamma, and

dead, I'd *like* my granddaughter to come to my graveside for such reason—because she is happy, so happy, to be meeting someone she loves, and with all those flowers in her arms. . . .

Christmas. The January snows. For two Sundays running, deep snowdrifts kept the Ponsonby family at home, and so the young Amelia did not see her beloved at all, for two whole weeks. Her heart was broken, she confided to her Journal; she longed for death. Not until January 26th, the day of the Special Service for the Poor of the Parish, would she get a chance to see him again. The days until that distant, magic date were numbered off in her journal like a count-down. Seven more days—six more days—five more days—and so on, down to "one".

And then—nothing. The great day, January 26th, comes and goes, and Amelia Caroline Ponsonby records of it not one word. Mr B. is never mentioned again.

Had the long-ago Amelia grown suddenly tired of him? Had he broken her heart in so dastardly a manner that she cannot bring herself to set his name on paper ever again?

The subsequent entries gave no clues, though from mid-February onwards the young lady was setting down plenty else. Fittings for dresses; a forthcoming visit to her cousins, the Honourable Ralph and his brother. A pony had strained its fetlock; Papa had been angry when some village children were caught throwing sticks in the paddock. More fittings for dresses.

Had Mr B. left the neighbourhood, perhaps? Taken another curacy elsewhere? Or had he—disaster of disasters—got married?

Amelia—Amelia Summers, that is—had at last to face the fact that she would never know. She skimmed through the book right to the very last page, but in vain. Mr B. had disappeared without trace, and forever.

It was nearly two o'clock in the morning by now, and Amelia's eyes were pricking with tiredness. Slowly, she began to close the leather covers, but as she did so a passage caught her eye that she must have missed. About halfway through it was, still in the era of Mr B.'s glory.

"O, Posterity, Posterity!" she read, the words dancing before her tired eyes. "Will you not spare a tear for one so young, so innocent, whose heart is broken? I shall not see him now until

Saturday! How can I live through the bleak waste of days and hours that separate me from my love?"

It was impossible to read any further. Amelia was quite cross-eyed with exhaustion. She switched off her lamp and lay back among her pillows, her eyes closing of their own accord.

. . . are you there, Amelia Caroline Ponsonby? This is Posterity speaking. I *did* shed a tear for you, just as you asked, but not at that particular paragraph, which I found a bit soppy, actually, though I daresay it was all right in those days. It was the bit about your grandmamma that made me cry, because now you *are* a grandmamma and dead; and I'm sure you never really thought you would be.

But the bit that made me cry the most was the *happy* bit, the bit where you asked Posterity, which is me, to share your great joy—and oh, I did, I did! Because I too have known the rare and wonderful joy of which you write, and maybe that is why I have been able to get in touch with you like this, across all these years: because we are both so happy. Maybe happiness is like that?

Or maybe it's because I'm called Amelia, too. Isn't that strange?

I wish I knew what happened to Mr B., but I suppose I never shall.

I hope you had a happy life, and got married and everything. Well, of course you did, or you couldn't be Dorothy's grandmother. . . .

The book slid from Amelia's fingers, and her mother, hearing the thud from her bedroom next door, tiptoed in just in time to to hear her daughter murmuring drowsily, "I dreamed I was Amelia!"

Identity-crisis? Ego-disorientation?

Peggy was thankful, at least, that Maureen Denvers wasn't here listening, or it would be all round the neighbourhood before the day was out that Peggy Summers was having teenage troubles at last, and wasn't managing so marvellously as a single parent after all.

55

CHAPTER VIII

SHYLY, AMELIA TOOK a step in the direction of the oval gilt mirror which (to her father's annoyance) Rita had insisted on propping up against one of the bookshelves, thereby at a single stroke replacing the entire works of Dostoevsky by her own smooth, delicately-moulded features.

"Well, where *can* I have it, then?" she'd demanded when Adrian registered his outrage.

"What about *here?*" he'd sulkily suggested, "what about *there* . . . ?" But either the light was wrong, or the plaster wouldn't take rawlplugs, or it would mean taking down Adrian's set of horse-brasses; and over the whole discussion had hung like a dark raincloud the fact that Adrian didn't want the damn thing anywhere. There was a mirror in the bathroom, wasn't there? And one alongside the shelf in the hall? Well, then.

Rita hadn't gone on arguing. She had begun to learn that Adrian's selfishness was a weapon which, in skilled hands, could often be used against him, and so she just kept putting the mirror where she wanted it, and moving it away again the moment he asked her to, until one of them got tired of it, which of course was him. Quietly, she notched up the victory, and went on to bigger things.

"There—have a look!" she now said to Amelia, motioning the child towards a chair in front of the mirror on its improvised dressing-table. "Sit down, and tell me how you like it"—and then she stood back, and watched, with a little flicker of triumph at the corners of her mouth, while Amelia turned her head this way and that, tossed the loose hair back and then let it fall forward again; at last allowing a wondering, incredulous smile to spread across her face.

"Oh . . . *Rita!*" was all she said; but it didn't really need words. They could both see with their own eyes that the sallow, rather small-featured face had been absolutely transformed by this frame of gleaming luxuriant hair, touched here and there with golden lights.

"A special shampoo for greasy hair, with conditioner," Rita

had ordained, with good-humoured firmness, brandishing the specially purchased bottles and escorting the dazed and as yet reluctant Amelia towards the bathroom. "You see, you first have to rub it in thoroughly—like this—and then . . . no, not like that! You have to *really* rinse it, three or four times, until the water runs absolutely clean. And then, if you fancy a few highlights—we mustn't overdo it, though, you're very young. . . ."

The blow-drier, of course, had been part of the magic. Mummy didn't have a blow-drier at home, and Amelia had never really come across one before, and at first she backed away a little warily. She didn't want to end up looking *silly*.

"My goodness, I couldn't *live* without my blow-drier!" Rita had cried—having already proved the point by leaving the thing around here, there and everywhere among Adrian's most treasured belongings, ever since she came here. "A blow-drier is an absolute *must*! You see, Amelia, your hair is very fine as well as greasy. It's *difficult* hair, and the worst thing you can possibly do with difficult hair is to dry it the way *you* do—crouched right up against an electric fire reading a book. It dries out all the oils and drains the colour. Now, with a blow-drier. . . ."

And now, looking in the mirror, Amelia could see that Rita had been absolutely right about absolutely everything. The stringy, damp-looking straggles of mouse were gone as if they had belonged to another life, and in their place fell these new, luxuriant locks which swung as she moved, full of bounce and highlights, flashes of blonde and chestnut setting off the pale, not-quite-straw colour of the whole.

Amelia could not speak. And when Rita approached with the suggestion of a broad blue band to hold the weight of hair back from her forehead, she just swallowed, and sat like Cinderella with the fairy godmother, letting the wonders happen.

She was beautiful! Well, practically. What *was* Daddy going to say!

She wriggled off the chair excitedly—and then paused, remembering that Daddy was cross. Not *very* cross, and no doubt she could get him out of it. In fact, she was sure she could, because she knew, in this case, exactly what it was that had made him cross. It had made *her* cross too, at the time, but then that had been before the magic transformation. It was like looking back on another world.

It was only an hour ago, actually; or maybe even less. She had burst into her father's flat a little before two, looking forward to a nice long afternoon of writing, reading and dreaming. She had a small amount of geography homework to finish first, though, and she decided to get it out of the way at once. Unpacking her school bag, she spreadeagled herself in her usual fashion on the carpet, with atlas, text-book and notes in front of her.

"Now, Amelia"—Rita's voice had broken into those very first minutes of concentration—"it's not worth getting out all those books just now. We're going out."

"*Out?*"

"*OUT?*"

The united outrage of father and daughter would have made most women quail.

"Yes, *out*," repeated Rita firmly. "It's terribly boring staying cooped up in here like this. And on such a lovely day! Look at it! The sun's come out! It's *spring!*"

There was a moment of stunned silence. Then:

"Oh *no*, Rita, *please!* Daddy and I *never* ..."

"Oh, now, Rita, for heaven's sake! I've *explained* to you that on Sundays I have to ..."

"'*Have to*!' To hell with 'have to'! I tell you, the sun's shining! The daffodils are out! Why, we could go to *Kew*...."

Kew. Kew was near Gunnersbury. And Gunnersbury, according to the fourth-form bush-telegraph, was where Mr Owen lived! Lived, alas, with his wife, but even so they might not spend *all* their time together. Maybe the wife was boring? Not his intellectual equal? Maybe he sought opportunities for getting away from her for an hour or two? What more likely than that he might decide to go for a walk in Kew Gardens by himself this bright afternoon? Wandering along the paths, musing gloomily, maybe, on the boring domestic scene to which he had so soon to return, he might suddenly chance to look up, and there, stepping lightly alongside a bank of daffodils, he would catch sight of ..."

"My *hair*!" had wailed Amelia despairingly at this point, "I haven't washed it for *days*! How can I go *anywhere* when my hair's all ..."

Her father had looked at her in amazement; Rita as a cat looks

58

at a whole roast chicken left miraculously unattended: and that was the way it began.

The hasty trip to the chemist's that was always open on Sundays: the earnest discussion with the girl about the exact shade and texture of Amelia's hair . . . and then . . . and then . . . the magic being set in motion.

"Daddy . . . Daddy, look!" she said now, coming a little hesitantly round the side of his desk.

"Look, Daddy, do you notice anything?"

"Ye Gods!" Adrian's astonishment was all Amelia could have hoped—perhaps indeed more, for to show himself so utterly dumbfounded at the fact that his daughter was looking pretty *could* have been interpreted an unflattering.

Amelia, however, did not interpret it thus. She giggled delightedly, and blushed a lovely rose-pink, thereby unwittingly completing the transformation.

Her father seemed quite at a loss for adequate comment. "Oh, I say, *chicken!*" was the best he could manage, and then he swept her into his arms in a great bear's hug.

Fifteen minutes later, they were all three in the car, on the way to Kew Gardens.

They didn't, of course, meet Mr Owen; but the first part of the afternoon was almost as exciting as if they had. Round every corner of the winding paths he might have appeared; in every one of the hot-houses he might have popped out from behind a great fern. Every heavily-built figure in the far distance might have turned out to be him as it approached; and every swarthy face with horn-rimmed glasses looked, for a millionth of a second, like his face.

For half an hour—for nearly three-quarters—these joys were sufficient. In front of budding azaleas Amelia posed herself hopefully, her new, wonderful hair lifting in the spring wind; beside beds of narcissus she loitered; and in among the bare, leafless birches of the bluebell wood—no bluebells yet, of course—she wandered expectantly, keeping all the time a few careful paces behind her father and Rita so as to give the impression of being alone. Lightly, driftingly, she stepped between the trees, putting spring into each step so that her hair would lift and bounce against her shoulders. A dryad, anyone of a literary turn of mind might have thought, a dryad dreaming her woodland dreams. . . .

But people of a literary turn of mind seemed to be thin on the ground that afternoon, no one looked at her at all. And though a number of men strolled past, some of them heavily-built and with shoulders hunched in thought, none of them were Mr Owen. Many of them were with their wives and families—and with sudden horror it occurred to Amelia that Mr Owen might have *children*, too! This was somehow far, far worse than a wife, it was unthinkable, and so Amelia stopped thinking about it.

Anyway, Daphne would be sure to have said if he had; she'd never have missed out on a tit-bit of news like that.

It was cold by the time they left the bluebell wood, the sun had begun to go down, and Amelia, who had refused to wear her thick winter coat because the collar of it got in the way of her hair swinging properly, was beginning to shiver. The strollers became fewer and fewer; Daddy was bored; Rita had turned silent. Amelia found herself weighed down by a growing certainty that the whole expedition was a failure; Mr Owen just wasn't here.

A little dispute blew up about tea. Rita wanted to have it here, in the tea-rooms; Adrian, huddled deep into his coat collar, wanted to go home, and soon. Amelia—who was quite as cold as her father, but had a superstitious feeling that if she suffered enough then the Fates might relent and make Mr Owen appear—took Rita's part, and they trailed back to the tea-rooms, only to find them closed.

"Went to Kew Gardens this afternoon. Mr Owen wasn't there."

Biro in hand, Amelia stared down at this bald, depressing little record of the day's non-event. How flat it was—how disappointing!—and as she re-read it, she became aware of something akin to rebellion arising in her soul. She was noticing now, for the first time, the horrid similarities between her own diary and that of her namesake more than a century ago:

Mr B. did not look in the direction of our pew this morning! Walked with Hester and Miss O. into the village, and back

60

and forth in front of the School several times, but still Mr B. did not appear. . . .

To think that after all these generations of progress, it was all just as difficult as ever! In spite of Permissiveness, and the Sexual Revolution and everything, nothing had changed!

It was ridiculous! It was humiliating! It wasn't to be borne! "Mr Owen wasn't there," indeed!

All at once, Amelia caught her breath; her eyes widened, and she stared unseeingly at the wall in front of her.

Then, bending once more over the sparsely-filled page, she began to write.

And write, and write, and write. She stopped only for tea, and for the drive home in the car; and that night, long after she should have been asleep, she was still sitting up in bed, writing, writing, writing.

CHAPTER IX

"Me *and* Rita, do you mean?" asked Adrian uneasily.
Motioning his secretary to withdraw, he then pressed the receiver
closer to his ear to make sure he had heard Derek Langley's invitation aright. "Both of us—or did you just mean . . . ?"

"I meant just *you*, Adrian, as a matter of fact," replied Derek,
a little diffidently. "The second person plural in English often
injects an element of embarrassment into these otherwise uncomplicated negotiations, does it not? In my opinion, we should have
retained the 'thou' of earlier times specifically for use on this type
of occasion. As it is, a certain crudity is forced upon me, in saying,
in so many words, 'No, I don't want you to bring your mistress
to dinner with me'—and yet this is what the deficiencies of our
Anglo-Saxon tongue compels me to say. So perhaps you'll allow
me to go back to the beginning, and repeat my invitation in the
more gracious style of an earlier age? Wilt thou, Adrian, come
on Friday the seventeenth, at about six-fifteen, to partake of a
modest meal such as a recently-abandoned husband may find himself able to provide? Perhaps, on some future occasion, I shall
have the pleasure of entertaining you and my wife together, but
just at this particular juncture, I feel it would be best if you and I
could have a word or two privately. Wouldn't you agree?"

A word or two. The phrase rarely means that the words are
going to be pleasant ones, let alone that the number of them will
not exceed two. A word or two about what, anyway?

The divorce, naturally. Adrian felt the beginnings of panic. He
had a wild, totally unreasonable urge to cry out, "For God's sake,
why *me*? It's none of *my* business!"—but of course this was such
nonsense that he himself wondered that a sane and intelligent
man could even have formulated the thought.

Because, of course, it *was* his business—more his business than
anybody's. He, Adrian, was the prime cause of the whole damn
mess-up—the whole realignment of their relationships on a more
realistic basis, he hastily corrected himself. It was he, and no one
else, who four years ago had fallen in love with Rita, had seduced

62

her, and had put into her receptive little head the idea of actually leaving the husband whom she had hitherto been content to complain about in her soft, non-stop little voice. Sometimes, looking back, Adrian wondered if he hadn't fallen in love with Derek's failings before he'd fallen in love with Rita herself. It does something for a man's ego to hear from a pretty woman about all the things another man can't do in bed, about the holidays he hasn't taken her on, the presents he hasn't given her, the words of love he's never murmured. Adrian had straightaway bought her a gold bracelet, told her he loved her, and taken her on holiday to Ibiza; and though she'd been ill with cystitis most of the time, and the hotel had cost more than twice as much as the brochure had indicated, and Peggy had found out about the whole escapade absolutely immediately, nevertheless it had still made Adrian feel no end of a fellow. Of course, Peggy didn't know about the cystitis, and Adrian was damned if he'd ever tell her about *that*; and the tears, the jealousy, and the sudden, belated passion she'd evinced on his return had seemed like the warmest welcome he'd received in years, and had gone far to soothe his bruised marital ego. He might be no great shakes at Ludo or at reading bedtime stories, but to be able to strut around for a season as the Casanova of Acacia Drive had temporarily quite made up for being such a rotten father all these years, and such a difficult, crotchety husband. He began to feel like a new man, neither difficult nor crotchety, and not forty-three, either.

It was a wonderful feeling, he wanted to hang on to it for ever; and of course Rita came as part of the package. *Was* the package, he'd hastily corrected himself; and after spending a couple more weekends with her—she was quite recovered by now—and taking her out to dinner and the theatre half a dozen times, he felt himself to be really in love. As, indeed, who wouldn't be, watching other men's heads turn in envy as he walked into restaurants with such a girl on his arm? Waiters greeted him as if he was a king, ushering him to the best tables, pulling chairs back with a flourish, and all because he had the Queen with him. Not the beauty queen, perhaps, but the Queen of whatever it is that makes this sort of thing happen.

And Rita never let him down. Always, when he took her out, she was flawlessly groomed, elegantly and expensively dressed on Derek's not inconsiderable salary, her face and hair aglow with skilled attention. She looked ravishing, and not a bit like Peggy, with her unadventurous perm and her "Should I wear my blue, Adrian, or my beige with the lace insets?" As the weeks went by Adrian, drunk with pride, became indiscreet to the point of lunacy, showing Rita off here, there and everywhere; to friends, colleagues, even neighbours; taking her deliberately to pubs and restaurants where they were bound to be recognised.

And in the end, it was all these friends and colleagues and acquaintances who, despite their mild and generalised disapproval, finally pushed him to the point of divorce. "What a smasher!" he could almost hear them thinking as he sailed with Rita through revolving doors and across lush carpets. "Fancy—old *Adrian!* Didn't know he had it in him!" And after a few weeks of this sort of thing, it dawned on him that any idea of dropping Rita had by now become absolutely untenable. The prospect of being seen, next time, with Peggy, in either her blue or her beige with the lace insets, was one which he simply could not contemplate: and indeed, why should he, Peggy being as snappy and ill-natured as she'd become of late?

Besides, he loved Rita. He really did. He loved the way she picked delicately and yet greedily at her food. He loved the slow way she'd lift those heavy eyelashes of hers and look at him long and thoughtfully before saying, "*You* choose, darling", when offered a choice of wines. She knew nothing about wines, any more than she knew anything about petroleum, or world affairs, or music, or even about holiday resorts or detective stories; but she had this lovely way of pausing, as if in deep thought, before saying No, I've never been there, no, I've never seen that, no, I don't read those kind of books, no, I've never heard of him. And after each of these admissions she'd give a sweet, enquiring little smile, one eyebrow lilting delicately upwards, as if the one thing she'd been waiting for all her life was for Adrian to tell her all about it, whatever it was.

"*Do* explain to me, darling, exactly what you *do* at this petroleum place," she'd say, and then sit gazing deep, deep into his eyes while he explained, and she didn't listen to one single word.

In fact, she was lovely. And if he ever *should* want a real, actual conversation with her, there was always the subject of Derek, and how he lost his erection every time the phone went, and left the cups and glasses upside down on the draining-board collecting smears, instead of drying them and putting them away at once.

You wouldn't do that, would you, darling, the huge, trusting eyes seemed to say; and, No, of course I wouldn't, his bemused smile would answer, dazzled and inattentive.

Wouldn't what? Luckily, she never asked. In those days, it wasn't her way to set this sort of trap for him, this was one of the nice things about her. Or else it was that she'd forgotten herself what it was they were talking about, her fluttering mind having already settled upon something else. Hell, what did it matter *which* it was? He loved her fluttering mind, so different from his own—not to mention from Peggy's, with its awful ability to remember word for word exactly what he'd said he was going to do last Wednesday week, and to compare it with what he now said he *had* done. He didn't like minds like that, not in women, anyway, unless, that is, the woman in question happened to be employed by him, in which case such a mind was of course essential.

And if, as that first wonderful autumn and winter went by, Rita's mind began to flutter just a little bit less, and even to show on occasion traces of a talent in no way inferior to Peggy's own for quoting back at him, word for word, exactly what he'd said in some quite different context weeks and weeks ago—well, by this time everything was amply compensated for by the fact that he was now having regular sex with her, sometimes at her place when Derek was out, and sometimes at his when Peggy was. The sessions at the Langleys' home in Wimbledon were slightly marred, from Adrian's point of view, by Rita's rather complicated brand of loyalty to her husband, which involved things like not drinking whisky out of the proper glasses, and Adrian's not lying on Derek's side of the double bed. It so happened that Adrian always preferred to have the woman on his left to start off with, so that his right arm could encircle her, and on the non-Derek side of the bed this manoeuvre became awkward if not impossible. It was the more annoying because, by all accounts, Derek didn't go in for much encircling at all, just in and out, Rita complained, and not even that if the telephone happened to ring.

At Adrian's home, on the other hand, there were other hazards, the chief one being his own constant dread that Peggy might walk in—or, even worse, Amelia. The fear was quite unrealistic; Amelia was at school, and Peggy (he always made one hundred per cent sure of this) safely spending the afternoon at her mother's, or at her pottery class, or some such activity of pre-arranged and inescapable duration. It was not that he suspected that Peggy might deliberately slip back and catch him unawares; such a trick would be quite alien to her character. Nor, when he really thought about it, did he seriously imagine that the pottery kiln might blow up, or his mother-in-law drop dead, or Amelia's school catch fire, necessitating a headlong and unforeseeable return home on the part of one or other of them in the early afternoon. As a scientist, he could see that the chances against any of these happenings were little short of astronomical. All the same, somewhere free-floating within this adult, rational brain of his still dwelt a child similar to that case-history little boy who wouldn't go to bed because he was frightened of witches.

"But witches aren't *real*, dear," the wise adults pointed out, to which the child replied: "It isn't a *real* witch that I'm frightened of."

This was exactly how Adrian felt. He *knew* that neither Peggy nor Amelia was going to walk in on him at half past two in the afternoon, but the picture of them doing so never left him.

Still, in spite of these drawbacks, it was all very enjoyable, even marvellous sometimes. As far as Adrian was concerned it could have gone on like this for ever, if Peggy hadn't suddenly, and without any warning, declared that she couldn't stand it any longer.

"Stand what?" had been Adrian's first astonished reaction— and his amazement had been genuine. So accustomed had he become to the routine of the thing that for the moment he'd completely forgotten that Peggy wasn't similarly accustomed; wasn't, indeed, supposed to know about it at all.

With an effort, Adrian forced his attention back to the present. Derek's voice was still going on and on down the telephone, explaining, in meticulous and utterly unnecessary detail, exactly how to get to Wimbledon, and about the one-way system which meant that you had to enter Winthrop Drive from the bottom end. Adrian had, of course, traversed the route in question something like a hundred times in the course of his affair with Rita, and for this very reason found it impossible to interrupt. Even to hint to his prospective host that he did not need all these directions seemed like the grossest piece of tactlessness, almost a breach of hospitality; and so he had to let the flow of superfluous information go on and on; and at dictation speed, too, so that he could pretend to be noting it down.

What a farce! Did Derek *really* imagine that the affair had never at any stage spread its tentacles as far as Wimbledon? Or was he, perhaps, going into all this rigmarole on purpose, out of some quiet, scholarly devilment of his own? There was no way of telling, nor of cutting short any part of the tedious pantomime. By the time it came to an end, Adrian's lips were quite dry with making little noises of assent and attentive co-operation.

"Friday the seventeenth, then," Derek finally repeated, in a tone indicating that he was at last bringing the thing to a conclusion, and with suitable expressions of gratitude, Adrian thankfully hung up; and having made a hasty note of the thing in his diary, he turned his attention back to his work.

At the time, nothing further in the way of preparation seemed to be necessary; but he found later that he had been guilty of a small but unfortunate oversight. Whether because of exceptional pressure of work that week, or whether it was some more subtle species of forgetfulness, it somehow came about that he omitted to tell Rita anything about the invitation at all, either that evening or the next. By the time Friday morning had come, and he still hadn't mentioned it to her, it really seemed like asking for trouble to do so, particularly since they'd had a row only the evening before, and were still barely recovered from it.

It had been about Rita's oval mirror again. Adrian, comfortably ensconced in his armchair, had been reaching behind him for his copy of *The Brothers Karamazov* to look up a certain passage; and on his knuckles encountering not the familiar worn leather bindings, but an upstart barrier of icy glass, he had whirled round in his chair, said "Bugger!" loudly, at the same moment as the mirror crashed to the floor in a hundred fragments.

"I *told* you not to put the bloody thing up there!" was the best he could manage in the way of apology to Rita for having broken one of her most cherished possessions; and Rita retaliated with tears, and accusations of having "done it on purpose!"; and if he'd only chuck half those bloody books away, then perhaps there might be a few inches of space in the flat that she could call her own; and what he saw in Dosto-bloody-effsky anyway she'd never understand, not if she lived for a hundred years.

The quarrel was cleared up in the end, of course, splinters of glass and all, but on the following morning—which was Friday—Rita was still wearing her sniffy, martyred look. Clearly, it was no morning for saying brightly over the breakfast table, "By the way, darling, your husband has invited me to dinner tonight, and has specially asked me not to bring you." It seemed to Adrian that it would be an altogether better thing to put the matter more gently, like Darling, there's a meeting of the Finance Committee this evening that I just have to go to . . . so don't wait up for me . . . I may be pretty late. . . .

Fancy having to tell lies like this about an assignation with a bloody *husband*! But there; it sometimes seemed to Adrian that life did just exactly what it liked with you, tossed you like a bit of driftwood just anywhere, simply for the fun of laughing at your contortions as you struggled comically back to safety.

CHAPTER X

SIX-FIFTEEN, DEREK HAD said; and as Adrian edged his car into the parking space in front of 22 Winthrop Drive, the evening light had already changed from gold to pink, and the first tinges of purple were creeping up over the roofs to the east. Derek must have been watching from the window, for he had the front door open before Adrian had finished locking the car. He stood there in the doorway, smiling hospitably, but not troubling to step an inch forward in welcome as his guest came through the gate, shutting and latching it behind him, and walked up the short gravel path towards the front door.

"This is very good of you—" began Adrian, as he drew near, and, "Not at all, it's a pleasure," Derek responded, and the two men shook hands.

"Or perhaps," amended Derek, " 'pleasure' is not quite the right word. 'Relief', perhaps, would be nearer the mark. Relief—as I am sure you will understand, Adrian—at the prospect of getting the whole thing tied up and settled at last. As to 'pleasure' "—by this time they were in Derek's comfortable, spacious front sitting-room, bathed just now in pinkish radiance through the big west windows—"as to pleasure, well, I take it that the whole business has been rather more fun for you than it has been for me? Wouldn't you say so? Now, what will you have, Adrian? Whisky? Vodka? Sherry . . . ?"

This time, of course, they were able to use the proper whisky glasses—and such had been his conditioning over the past four years that Adrian felt for a moment quite ill with guilt as his fingers closed round the fine crystal. He'd never felt guilty like this when lying with Derek's wife in Derek's double bed—on the non-Derek side of it, of course.

"Well—to you and my wife!" said Derek, raising his glass, and Adrian, perforce responding, wondered if Derek had deliberately chosen so uncomfortable a toast, or was it just a momentary piece of clumsiness?

There was no way of telling. The man was smiling pleasantly, offering no clues. He sat facing the window, and the pink sunset light give his thin, rather ascetic face an unwonted glow of buoyant health and well-being, and he sipped his drink with an air of almost sybaritic enjoyment, though never once taking his eyes off Adrian's face. Again Adrian felt uncomfortable, and again could pin down no precise reason for it. Presently, Derek set down his glass and cleared his throat.

"I expect," he began, "that you've been wondering why, exactly, I've invited you round this evening?"—and then, in response to Adrian's small deprecatory murmur, he hastily amended: "Of course, my dear fellow, I don't mean to imply . . . that is, I am of course delighted to have you here in any case—only too delighted. Any time. But I was referring to my particular reason for inviting you—by yourself, without my wife—on this particular evening. You haven't wondered about it, then? Not at all? As you came along in the car, for instance . . . ?"

Again, there was something just slightly—not provocative, exactly, that would be too strong a word—but something conducive to discomfort rather than comfort about the man's choice of words. Why, for instance, did he have to keep saying "my wife" instead of "Rita"? Of course, she *was* his wife still, in law, but all the same one would have thought that, on a social occasion like this, ordinary tact and good manners would have suggested . . .

But the alert, lightish eyes, fixed so intently on Adrian's face, had no hostility in them, only a detached, almost childlike curiosity. Why, the fellow just wanted an answer to his question—it was as simple as that!

"No, to be quite honest with you," Adrian replied, "I didn't wonder at all. Should I have? It seemed to me a most sensible idea that you and I should get together and try to work out between us—without upsetting Rita, that is, or getting involved in any sort of acrimony—that we should try to work out—well, you know. Like finances. That sort of thing."

The question of what, if any, maintenance Rita was entitled to from Derek, and whether, in law, any of it would survive the fact of her co-habiting (the word "marriage" Adrian still wasn't facing) with Adrian, had not yet been mentioned. And it would be nice to know. Not that Rita's quite reasonable salary from her receptionist's job wasn't an adequate contribution to their joint finances, but it would be useful to know her actual rights. One wouldn't necessarily—or even probably—insist on them: poor old Derek had had a pretty raw deal as it was, without being expected to pay for it as well. Still, an accurate knowledge of the actual facts of any situation can never be other than an advantage.

"Oh, *finances*!"—Derek brushed the word aside with an actual sweep of the arm, as if it were a speck of dust on the polished table in front of him. "*Finances*! Oh, I wouldn't worry about finances, old chap. Rita will get what she wants out of you, just as she will out of me, don't you worry. *She* won't need any of these lawyer-Johnnies to tell her how to get her pretty little claws on your salary. *Or* mine. . . ."

Adrian was taken aback. Was *this* the Poor Derek whose tender sensibilities had to be considered at every turn? Was *this* the kindly, super-tolerant husband who loved his wife so much that he would put up with any and every humiliation rather than lose her companionship?

Adrian tried to pass it off lightly.

"Yes, well, I expect the lawyers *will* have something to say on the money question, because they always do, don't they? But if *you're* not bothered about that side of things, and *I'm* certainly not, then it shouldn't be too traumatic. So let's leave it for the moment. It's the actual divorce, I suppose, that we have to discuss. I'm perfectly willing, naturally, to be cited as co-respondent. . . ."

Derek seemed to be only half attending.

"Co-respondent?" he repeated vaguely. "Oh, my dear chap, I don't think they have co-respondents any more. I don't *think* they do. It's 'irreversible breakdown' that's the thing now. I *think* it is. Not that I care. She can get rid of me any way she likes."

Adrian felt a stab of compassion for the man's obvious bitterness, but he was irritated as well. Things were difficult enough already, and Derek's continuing misery was a burden he could well do without. He felt guilty, put-upon and inadequate, and he suddenly longed to punch Derek's face, hard, right in the middle of those controlled, scholarly features.

As so commonly happens, such a turmoil of conflicting emotions tends to find expression in a weak trickle of clichés.

"Yes, well, I expect it'll all work out in the end," said Adrian, draining the last of his whisky at a gulp. "No use crossing our bridges till we come to them, eh? We can only do our best. And we must remember it's Rita's happiness we really have to think of. After all, both of us, in our different ways . . ."

"*Rita's* happiness? My dear fellow, we don't have to worry about *that!* Rita is always happy when she's destroying something. She spent nearly seven years destroying me, and happy all the time —didn't she tell you? Oh, I'm sure she did, she told everyone: how the first few years of our marriage were quite idyllic? Well, I'm sure that for her they were so, there was nothing left of me at the end of them, nothing at all. And that, of course, was where the trouble started. Having destroyed me utterly, she was up against a bit of a dead end. She was like an artist with no more canvasses left to work on. . . ."

Refilling his glass, he held it up to the dying light, staring into it long and pensively, the flickers of gold reflected faintly on his lined, intelligent face.

"She has this talent for destruction, you see," he explained thoughtfully, "and, like all talents, it clamours to be used." Again he gazed deeply, abstractedly into the golden depths in front of his eyes. "For it *is* a talent, you know, Adrian, this power of turning to blackness and poison everything you touch. Like every artist, Rita needs scope for the exercising of her gifts; without it, she becomes frustrated. And this, Adrian, is where *you* come in. . . ."

"Now, look here . . . I say . . . !" Adrian helped himself, un-asked, to another neat whisky, and sat for a moment quite at a loss how to continue. He knew well enough—none better—how cruel, how bitter, how downright evil can be the things which otherwise ordinary, pleasant couples can say to and about each other when in the throes of divorce. At such a time, there are no holds barred, the sky is the limit where mutual vituperation is concerned. All the same, had he himself, even at the blackest moments, ever said anything half as awful as this about Peggy? Or she about him? He was sure they hadn't. On the other hand, had he—or Peggy either, for that matter—ever felt quite as miserable about the break-up of *their* marriage as Derek was obviously feeling about his? Misery on this sort of scale was something that Adrian hadn't encountered before; it embarrassed him.

Still, he must say *something*. He couldn't let these outrageous aspersions on the woman he loved—*had* loved, anyway—go unchallenged. The whole thing was further complicated, of course, by the fact that he was at this moment a guest in Derek's house.

"Look here, I say—" he began again"—you can't—I mean, Derek, you really *can't*—talk like that about anybody. I know you've had a rotten deal and all that, but there are limits! I realise you don't really mean it, but all the same it's not fair on Rita for you to go around saying . . ."

"Not *fair*? On *Rita*? When did I ever say I wanted to be *fair* to Rita? I said I wanted to *keep* her, but that's quite different, as I'm sure you'll be the first to agree. . . . But come, my dear fellow, enough of this! Before the light is quite gone, I want to show you my garden. Not a big garden, but quite interesting in its way. . . ."

Normally, there was nothing Adrian hated more than being shown round people's gardens, and particularly if they were "interesting "ones. This meant, in Adrian's experience, that they were full of things like half-dead dandelions from somewhere in Tibet, or meagre little globs of foliage encircling a thing like a dried lentil, only blue. And if you made an effort and said the slightest nice thing about it, then you'd get shown its photograph as well, on a colour slide, as soon as you got indoors. On top of which, in this particular case, he'd seen the garden hundreds of time already, from Rita's bedroom window. Not that he'd taken it in that much —a lot of miscellaneous greenery, as far as he could remember, interspersed by funny-looking shrubs. Probably they *were* from Tibet if the truth were known, but thank goodness Rita knew absolutely nothing about any of them, and so hadn't been able to tell him.

However, on this occasion, Adrian submitted to the impending ordeal with something like alacrity. He appreciated Derek's effort to change the subject, to pull himself together, and to rescue them both from the embarrassment of all that emotional stuff. By the time they got back indoors, they'd have recovered their usual guarded but nevertheless civilised relationship. For this, it was worth while enduring a spell of moderate boredom. It couldn't last long, anyway, because twilight was already at hand. Resignedly, Adrian set down his glass, hoisted himself from his comfortable chair, and followed his host across the hall to the door with Edwardian-style stained glass panels which led into the garden. Derek undid the creaking bolts slowly, and with a clumsiness which seemed somehow out of character; and then, with a sort of flourish, he threw open the door.

Adrian stared, absolutely stupefied. He had known, of course, that "interesting" gardens are liable to contain largish areas of bare earth broken only by little prison-encampments of stakes enclosing, with loving totality, some small and bewildered expatriate from distant peak or blazing desert "... the Lesser Something-Something from the Outer Hebrides ..." "a special minature variety that is only found in Iceland ... if you come next year, or the year after, you'll see ..."

Yes, areas of bare earth, and mingy, unenthusiastic plants he had expected: but *this* ...! He gazed unbelievingly. The whole garden was completely bare, lifeless and black, as if it had been swept by a death-ray. Not a green leaf, not a blade of grass anywhere.

Adrian turned to his host in bewilderment.

"What ...?" he begun helplessly; and Derek answered without looking at him, staring out expressionlessly over his domain of death.

"She only *meant* to poison my Mecanopsis superba," he explained deprecatingly. "She knew I loved them, you see. It's a special variety of poppy you know, from Bhutan in the Himalayas. I'd been working for years to get them acclimatised, and for the first time they were beginning to flower and propagate themselves. She meant the weed-killer just for them, but you know what a little scatterbrain she is; she didn't read the instructions on the container properly, and managed accidentally to poison the whole garden—roots, soil, the lot. Probably, it will never recover in my lifetime. Silly little thing, isn't she? Quite hopeless when it comes to anything practical. ...

"And now, my dear fellow, let us go in and eat. As you observe, there is not a lot to be seen out here, and anyway the light is going.

"I hope you like liver and bacon? It's the only thing I've really learned how to cook so far—I suppose, in my own way, I'm just as hopeless when it comes to anything practical as Rita is!"

He laughed, as if well pleased with his own humour, then turned and led Adrian indoors and into the dining-room.

74

CHAPTER XI

"BUT DADDY'S *always* here on Sundays!" cried Amelia, staring incredulously. "I've *never* got here and not found him!"

Had she been less engrossed in her own disappointment, Amelia would have noticed the fury, quickly controlled, which flickered across Rita's face at this futile protest. Futile, because how could *Rita* summon Daddy out of thin air—Rita who, if the truth were known, was a hundred times more agitated about Adrian's disappearance than Amelia, utterly confident of her secure and permanent place in his heart, could begin to imagine. And had Amelia been older, as well as less self-absorbed, she would have recognised the moment she came into the room that unmistakable look on Rita's face—the look of a woman who knows, or suspects, that her lover has at last really left her, and that this time he will not come back.

But Amelia, being only thirteen, was oblivious of all this. She was concerned only with the disruption of her own afternoon.

"But where *is* he?" she persisted, unwittingly rubbing salt into a red, raw wound that was beyond the range of her comprehension. "Where did he say he'd gone? When will he be back?"

No woman in Rita's situation is ever willingly going to admit to it—certainly not to a thirteen-year-old. The sordid truth—that Adrian had simply not come home either last night or the night before; that he had furthermore pretended (Rita had checked this with his secretary) that on Friday he'd been kept late at the office when he hadn't; and had thereafter stayed away the whole weekend without even bothering to telephone—all this added up to a picture so humiliating, as well as so drearily commonplace, that almost any woman would have tried to keep it secret.

Certainly Rita intended to.

"Your father's been called away on business, if you want to know," she snapped. "I expect he forgot all about you."

Let her have it right between the eyes, the smug little devil! Let *her* have a taste of being unwanted, rejected, let down; of having her love and loyalty slapped back into her face like a wet fish!

While Amelia's countenance slowly paled, a small flicker of satisfaction came into Rita's. The two stood staring at each other, in open enmity for the very first time. Suddenly, it was frightening.

Amelia took a step backwards.

"I'll go and ask Dorothy!" she exclaimed, turning on her heel. "*Dorothy* will know!"—and a moment later she was clattering downstairs at top speed, flight after flight, round the bends of the landings, till she reached the haven of the familiar basement kitchen.

"Dorothy will know!" In other words, "Dorothy, not Rita, is the one he's likely to have confided in!" Alone in the big room, Rita stood quivering, like a well-trained gun-dog waiting for some special signal. She was waiting for her lover, just as she had waited all the weekend, and by now she was feeling quite sick with longing for his return.

Because how can you punish adequately a man who just doesn't show up?

"Let me see; Friday. That's when I saw your Dad last, the Friday morning," said Dorothy, burrowing eagerly into his new drama like a rabbit excavating a cosy home for itself in some promising hillside. "Yes, he was just off to work, about nine o'clock it must have been, because that was the morning the builders were here, having a look round the Squatters' Flat. Four hundred pounds it's going to cost me, but Mr Hudson thinks we might get the Council to pay some of it. Squatters are their responsibility really, he says, and I might be entitled to some damages."

It was the ground-floor flat that Dorothy was talking about, the one on street level. Even though it was several weeks now since the squatters had cleared out—speeded on their way by awkward enquiries from Social Security about their entitlement to Supplementary Benefit—Dorothy still spoke of the flat—and indeed thought of it—as the Squatters' Flat, and no doubt would continue to do so until some new incumbent arrived to impregnate the place with his or her new name. So far, this hadn't happened, because the squatters had left it in such a state, and it had taken weeks of phone calls to get the builders even to come and give an estimate.

My goodness, what a business it had all been, one way and another! It still gave Dorothy a funny feeling when she thought about it, and especially when she recalled the way in which it had all come about. When the squatters had first arrived—in ones and twos, with rosy, guileless young faces and no luggage, she had taken for granted that they were visitors for one or other of the existing tenants. She hadn't at first given it a moment's thought, for was this not Liberty Hall, as she had so often boasted? People were in and out all the time, often staying the night as well, and Dorothy prided herself on asking no questions and making no fuss about such goings-on. And so thus it came about that only when the newcomers had established themselves eleven strong in the ground-floor flat, had changed the locks and had started cheeking her through the back windows when she went out to hang up the washing—only then did Dorothy begin to realise exactly what she was up against, and also how little, within the limits of the law, she could do about it. Her friends, naturally, had been highly indignant on her behalf—Adrian, in particular, volunteering to beat up the lot of them with his own hands. But that, of course, would have been "assault", and Dorothy naturally didn't want her only reliable tenant dragged off to prison at such a time.

And in fact, it gradually became clear to the onlookers that no such drastic knight-errantry was called for. Before long, Dorothy was referring to "My Squatters" with a note of pride in her voice, positively boasting about them among the neighbours as if they were a sort of status symbol, an authentic hallmark of the sort of trendy, telly-based with-it-ness to which she had always so wistfully aspired.

"Well, Dorothy, I hope it's taught you a lesson!" Adrian had said severely, after the thing had finally spluttered to its ignominious end. "I've always *said* you were crazy to keep that back door unlocked at all hours so that just anybody can walk in whenever they like! It's *asking* for trouble—didn't I always tell you so?"

And Dorothy, gazing at him respectfully, hadn't really known what to reply. Because, of course, it *had* taught her a lesson: it had taught her that even at sixty-seven, life can still be full of adventures and surprises: and if they could sometimes cost you four hundred pounds—well, so could a holiday in the South of France, and this way you escaped all that oily food and picking up stomach-bugs.

It was difficult to put into words, though; you could never explain it to someone as clever as Mr Summers, and so Dorothy didn't try. She just went on leaving the back door unlocked just as she'd always done. It was easier on her feet, for one thing. People could just come in and dump the laundry or the groceries or whatever on to the kitchen table without her having to stir from her chair: nor did she have to drag herself out of bed late at night to let in people who'd forgotten their keys.

"And you're *sure* that was the last time Daddy was here?" Amelia was asking anxiously. "On the Friday morning? And he didn't seem —you know—as if anything had happened? He didn't say anything about going away, or anything? Because that's what I can't understand. Rita says he suddenly had to go on a business trip—but then, why didn't he ring up? He *always* rings us up—me or Mummy—if anything like that happens!"

Dorothy shook her head enigmatically. She was torn between a real desire to comfort the child and a bounding hope that something exciting might have gone wrong.

"Yes, well, dear, it is a bit of a puzzle, I grant you," she said. "I wish I could tell you that I knew the answer, but I don't. He didn't say anything to *me* about any business trip! And he would, you know, if he knew he had anything like that coming up. He always does. He's very considerate, is your Pa—well, in those sort of ways, anyway. No, dear, I'll tell you what *I* think—" —here Dorothy leaned closer, lowering her voice to a confidential murmur —"*I* think they've had a quarrel! Your Pa, I mean, and *Her*! A real, dreadful row I reckon they've had—in fact, I *know* they have! I heard them, the Thursday night—broken glass and all sorts! She's not right for him, dear, that Rita isn't. Not for a clever gentleman like your Pa, she's just not in his class, I've always said so. Right from the start, when I first set eyes on her, I said ..."

"Oh, Dorothy, *please* ...!" begged Amelia, jigging about in her impatience. "*Please* help me decide what I'd better do! You see, even if it *was* a quarrel and all that, like you say, I still don't see why he couldn't have told *me* about it! I can see why he mightn't want Mummy to know, but he could still have told *me*! Or left me a note, or *something*! He must have *known* how worried I'd be, coming here like this and finding him just not there!"

"Yes, well, love, I know, it's a shame, and it's hard that *you* should be the one to suffer, in your innocence. But that's life for you; and the truth is that when a man and a woman start quarrelling like those two did that Thursday night—well, I'm afraid that that's where commonsense flies out of the window, and consideration for

78

anyone else, too—and they might do *anything*, either one of them. And you do have to remember that your Pa—I'm sure you won't mind my saying this, dear—your Pa does have a temper, and there's no sense denying it. If that woman up there was to have provoked him that little bit too far—and she's just the type, let me tell you—well, if something like that was to have happened, then I wouldn't be surprised if your Pa mightn't have walked right out on her, then and there, slamming the door behind him. And I wouldn't blame him either, it'd be no more than she deserves, the two-faced, stuck-up little. . .!

"But don't you worry, love, he'll be back. Any minute now, I wouldn't be surprised. He'd never be letting you down over this Sunday afternoon business, that's for sure. He thinks the world of you, dear, you know that, and he'd have to be dead and in his grave before he'd . . .

"There! What was that? I do believe that's your Dad now, just coming in the front door!"

But it wasn't. A race up the basement stairs revealed to Amelia's disappointed eyes nothing more exciting than Kathy and the baby, the latter wrapped up in layer after layer of wool and blanketing against the soft spring sunshine, and screwing up its face in small displeasure at each of the bumpety-bumpings that marked the progress of the push-chair down the front steps. Amelia hurried to Kathy's help, less from any very highly developed urge to be obliging than as an excuse for getting into conversation and at the same time having a good look right to the end of the road for signs of her father's car.

There were none; and turning to her companion, who was at that moment wrapping yet another blanket round her muffled-up charge, ventured to ask if she'd seen anything of Adrian this weekend?

Kathy looked up, with the glazed half-comprehension of one whose mind is far, far away.

"Adrian. . .? Oh, Mr Summers. Your father. I'm afraid I never noticed, Amelia, I've been in such a—well, you know! And while we're on the subject, well, not exactly, but you know what I mean—I suppose *you* haven't seen anything of my Brian, have you? On your way here from the bus-stop, I mean? He popped out for some ciggies just after breakfast, and he was going to come straight back

... and it's gone two now. I just wondered if, when you were passing the Shipton Arms, perhaps....?

Amelia shook her head. The two girls stood for a moment, staring into each other's eyes with a sort of mutual recognition. At this moment, they were both members of the dreariest club in the world, anxiety its badge, and insecurity its membership card.

"Oh, well—thanks," they both said, and with weak, despondent smiles they parted, Kathy to trundle her baby round the local pubs and hot-spots in search of Brian, and Amelia to mount guard at the foot of the steps.

There were still no signs of her father's car; and after twenty minutes or so, cold, bored and disappointed, she wandered back indoors again. As she neared the top of the stairs, she quickened her pace, in the vague and implausible hope that her father might have reappeared in her absence, despite the watch she'd been keeping at the street door.

He hadn't, of course; but Rita, rather to Amelia's surprise, seemed to have quite recovered her good humour, so much so that she even suggested another hair-washing session like last week, blow-drier and all. Though slightly taken aback, Amelia acquiesced readily enough; it was at least a way of passing the time until Daddy turned up. And afterwards, brushing out the silky, gleaming locks, Rita was struck by a further brilliant idea.

"Amelia! Listen, I've just thought of something! Why don't you let me do your nails for you? Properly, I mean, with pink nail-varnish like I do mine? Or maybe something a bit paler would look better at your age ... let me see what colours I've got...."

She began rootling in her big, untidy box of make-up, which stood, as usual, spilling its contents on to Adrian's polished walnut chess-table. Amelia watched open-mouthed, half aghast and half thrilled at the revolutionary proposition. What would they say at school? What would Mr Owen think when he glanced over her shoulder to see how she was getting on with her work, and suddenly noticed ...

"But aren't I too young?" she suggested shyly; and then listened, agog with willing credulity, while Rita assured her that no, of course she wasn't too young. Lots of girls of thirteen—even twelve— paint their nails nowadays. Naturally, Rita wouldn't recommend anything too sophisticated, like crimson or orange; but she'd got here a lovely pale rose-colour which would be just exactly right. It wouldn't be too noticeable, and yet it was amazing the difference it could make to the whole look of your hands. . . .

That Amelia's hands could do with something amazing happening to them could hardly be doubted. Inky, stubby, and with unevenly bitten nails . . . Rita set to work on this unpromising material with both skill and patience, gently pushing back the cuticles, filing down the rough edges, and even achieving some sort of rounded shapeliness in the case of those nails which weren't too severely bitten.

"It's a pity we're having to make them so short," murmured Rita, bending over her work. "We could have shaped them into really pretty ovals if only you didn't bite them so much. Still, it *has* made a difference, hasn't it? Now, then. . . ." and a minute or two later she was embarked on the final and most exciting stage of the whole operation: painting on the colour.

Amelia watched, fascinated. It was obvious that Rita had a real talent for this sort of thing, and it was enthralling to see how the delicate little pink-tipped brush followed with its feather-touch the exact curve of each nail, shaping the paler half-moons with expert care.

Little finger . . . fourth finger . . . middle finger—and then, suddenly, the whole room rocked to a violent slam of the door, which sent the little brush skittering in pink zig-zag streaks right across Amelia's hand.

"Leave that child alone!" Adrian was shouting, from right across the room. "Leave her alone! Let go of her hand instantly! Don't touch her! I won't have you touch her!"—and a moment later he was across the room and gathering his shocked and bewildered young daughter into his arms.

CHAPTER XII

"WHAT I SHALL never understand, Adrian, is how you could be such a *fool*," Rita was expostulating later that evening, when they were at last on their own. "Fancy you, a grown man, letting poor Derek stuff you up with all those fantasies and lies! Don't you realise he's mad? Not properly, mental-hospital mad, I don't mean—just mad where *I'm* concerned. It's ever since he found out about *you*, actually, Adrian, it really seemed to send him round the bend for a while, and since then, every so often he gets fits of being downright paranoic about me. When he's like that he'll accuse me of just any crazy thing that comes into his head. This weed-killer nonsense, for example; it's typical."

"You mean you *didn't* do it, then?" By now, Adrian was beginning to feel quite at sea, and did not know what to believe. Derek's quiet, bitter revelations had been painfully convincing at the time; but now here was Rita being equally convincing to the contrary. What she said was perfectly plausible; a man as hurt and humiliated as Derek appeared to have been might well over-react to minor disagreements and mishaps, building them up in his mind into something quite out of proportion to the original facts.

On the other hand, he, Adrian, had seen the black, devastated garden with his own eyes. He would never forget the shock, the sense of nightmare, that had overwhelmed him in those first seconds. If Rita hadn't done it, then who had?

"You mean—" he started again carefully "—you mean, Rita, that it wasn't you who put weed-killer on the things at all? Not at any time?"

"Oh. Well. . . ." Rita pouted, and made a little face. "Well, naturally, I used weed-killer now and again, everyone does, you have to, to keep the weeds under. And poppies *are* weeds. They're *wild* flowers, and wild flowers are *weeds*. Anyone knows *that*!"

"I see. And so—now, let's get this straight, Rita—you admit now that you *did* put weed-killer on them, just as Derek said . . .?"

Rita made an angry little movement.

"Oh, well, Adrian, if you're going to start taking Derek's side

against me . . .! I tell you I used the wretched stuff for weeds—
damn it all, that's what it's for! That's why it's called 'weed-killer'!
Is it my fault that the whole damn garden was weeds . . .? It was a
disgrace to the neighbourhood, I was ashamed to take anyone out
there! I wanted a *proper* garden, Adrian—with geraniums and
things!"

The little-girl pathos of this modest aspiration might have won
over Adrian totally and brought the quarrel to an end then and
there, if Rita hadn't at that same moment recalled her other, and
far more substantial, grievance. She turned on him agrily.

"Where the hell have you *been*, anyway? And why, in the name
of common decency, didn't you tell me you were going to Derek's
in the first place? Then I could have come with you, and none of
this would have happened. Here I've been, going mad with worry
the whole weekend, and you never even bothered to phone me! It's
worse than being married to Henry VIII—he did at least take the
trouble to let his wives know before he cut their heads off!"

In vain did Adrian point out that he *wasn't* planning to cut
Rita's head off, and that actually she wasn't his wife either; this
well-meant attempt to put the argument on a more logical basis
simply seemed to make matters worse. So he apologised yet again
for his thoughtlessness in not phoning; and explained once more
that his mind had been in such a turmoil after the evening with
Derek that he'd "just kept driving around".

What, for two days on end?

Adrian sighed and realised that there was no other option than
to tell her the truth: how, on a sudden, desperate impulse he had
turned the car southwards and gone to visit Rita's mother in Kent.

"*Mummy*! But you couldn't have!" shrieked Rita. "She doesn't
even know you exist!"

"Well, she does now," said Adrian complacently. "In fact, she
appears to have known about me all along, despite your efforts.
She seemed very pleased, actually. She says she's been wanting
to meet me and have a talk for years. She says . . ."

"But Adrian! She *can't* have! She thinks I'm still happily
married to Derek. . . . That's why we had to go through with that
awful birthday party. So she wouldn't suspect anything . . ."

"Yes, she told me," agreed Adrian. "She says she thought you
carried it off very well, all things considered. And the way you
kept the guests from finding out about the garden—she thought

that was masterly. Though of course it did make it easier it being such a wet day, and dusk before they arrived. The closely-drawn curtains at every window made it look very cosy, your mother said, though of course *she* knew what you were hiding. We talked quite a bit about that garden, actually; that was what I went down for originally, to get her angle on it; sort of check on Derek's story, you know. And she told me that yes, you were like that, always had been; and she'd come to the conclusion that you couldn't help it. She told me that once, when you were about eleven, your grand-mother came to stay, bringing her beloved budgerigar with her. And . . ."

Rita burst into loud and furious sobbing, beating her fists on the table.

"I might have known it! You hate me! You want to stir up my enemies against me! You've spent the whole weekend listening to filthy lies about me, and enjoying it all so much you couldn't even drag yourself away for a moment to telephone and say where you were! I haven't slept for two nights, I've almost worried myself into a nervous breakdown about you! My god, I wish you *had* been with another woman, or dead, or all the things I've been thinking! I wish you'd crashed the car . . . !"

"So do I," said Adrian with sudden, uncharacteristic bitterness. "Then my poor little Amelia would at least have been spared . . ."

" *'Your poor little Amelia'!* That's all you think about, isn't it? Not 'poor little Rita', is it? What *she* suffers doesn't count! But I'm glad to hear that you're ashamed anyway. So you should be! Making an exhibition of yourself like that in front of your own daughter, and all because you couldn't bear to see the two of us having a good time together, without you! It's jealousy, that's what it is, Adrian; plain, spiteful jealousy. You can't bear to see your precious Amelia showing any affection for anyone but yourself! You were hoping she'd despise me, weren't you? That she'd look down on me for not being so bloody clever as you two are, for not having read all those bloody books and not being able to quote all that bloody poetry! It didn't occur to you, did it, that we might find ways of getting on together which had nothing to do with being clever . . . ? Interests which you can't share, and which shut you out in the cold? That's come as a shock to you, hasn't it? You were hoping for the good old stepmother thing, weren't you—both of us fighting over you, wounding one another, while your ego

84

grew fat on our blood! *I* know you, Adrian, I've known you for years; just one great bloated ego with a cheque-book ...!"

Adrian made no attempt to refute these charges. Instead, he passed his hand across his eyes in a gesture of utter weariness. Couldn't she shut up about it all? Hadn't they had enough for one evening? He was indeed ashamed of his uncontrolled outburst this afternoon, and the look of incredulous shock it had brought to his daughter's face. It was awful. Still, no one could say that he hadn't done what he could to make amends. He had apologised, he'd hugged and kissed the child, explaining to her that he'd been tired —worried—up all night; that he'd always had this peculiar aversion to nail-varnish, especially on very young girls ... that he didn't want her to grow up too soon ... to miss what can be the best part of childhood. ... He told her everything, in fact, which his quick and fertile intelligence could assemble at short notice, except the plain truth, for this was something that he could not tell to anyone: how the sudden sight of Rita, curved like a crow over the body of his precious daughter, peck-peck-pecking at it with little dabs of movement, had filled him with a blind, primitive terror and revulsion which even now he could not understand, and would certainly never divulge, not to anyone in the wide world.

Amelia had listened, quiet and non-committal, to his hastily assembled barrage of explanations. How much of it she had actually believed, he had no idea, but she had made no attempt to call his bluff, either then or later. On the drive home she asked no questions, indeed she spoke hardly at all; but then they often didn't speak much, he and she, both of them being given to spells of profound and concentrated thinking. It didn't mean there was anything amiss between them. By next Sunday, the whole thing would have blown over. These things do.

They do, that is, if only people will let them, and not go on and on and on about them. It seemed to Adrian that the whole of the rest of the evening, after Amelia's departure, was filled with Rita's voice— actually, physically filled with it, the way whole valleys can be filled with the sound of a waterfall.

"... and after all I've done for the miserable little creature, trying to make her look a little bit less hideous for your sake—

and *now* what sort of thanks do I get? 'Don't touch her!' you screech at me! D'you think I've got death-ray fingers, or something? Do I sting, like a scorpion? Or is it something more like leprosy I've got? Are you thinking that by my very presence I shall pollute your pure, innocent little daughter?

"Let me tell you something, Adrian: that sly, mealy-mouthed little Miss Innocent of yours wouldn't half take some polluting! She has a mind like a cesspool! That foul-mouthed old hag downstairs has done her work well—didn't I warn you? Unless, of course, your darling daughter's filthy mind is—what's the word?—like you were saying about short sight?—Genetic! That's it. Unless it's genetic. . . ."

Adrian's pretence of not listening could be maintained no longer. "Rita! Shut up! Stop it! Don't you dare tell me . . ."

"*Tell* you? My dear Adrian, I wouldn't waste the breath! You don't listen. You've trained yourself for years not to listen—pity there's not a degree in it!

"But don't worry, Adrian dear: although you can't listen, you *can* read—*that* you've made evident enough, evening after evening! And so if you'd rather read the evidence I've collected for you than listen to it, then read it you shall! Here—" she bent, and began scrabbling in the basket that stood by her chair "—here, let me show you what I found. . . ."

CHAPTER XIII

AMELIA, MEANTIME, WAS toying sulkily with the
Sunday supper Peggy had cooked—chips, beans and bacon, usually
firm favourites. But this time, she was finding it heavy going. She
had no appetite; and the conversation, too, was laborious.

"All right" and "Nothing much" were all she had so far found
to say about the terrible and dramatic afternoon: and it was lucky
that Peggy was by now so used to these laconic, not to say downright rude, responses to her Sunday evening questions, that she
attached little significance to them, and probed the matter no
further.

Which was a mercy; for nothing in the world would have
induced Amelia to reveal to anyone at all—least of all to her
mother—that awful scene of her father's humiliation.

For that was how she saw it. It wasn't his irrational display of
rage—incomprehensible though she had found it—which made
her feel ashamed for him; rather, it was the lies which had followed.

Not that Amelia was against lying in principle. She had read
J. S. Mill on the subject, and extracts from G. E. Moore, and
was inclined to agree with these authors that lying and not lying
are largely matters of social convention; and this was what Daddy
had seemed to think, too, when she'd discussed it with him one
afternoon.

So it was not the fact of his lying to her that had hurt, but
rather his helpless, despairing air of having been driven to it. He
was lying not voluntarily, and of set purpose, but under some
awful compulsion. Her strong, self-sufficient, imperturbable father
was suddenly diminished in her eyes, it was as if some power had
gone out of him. For the first time in her life, she found herself
having to feel sorry for him.

No, *not* for the first time; and this, in a way, was what made
the thing so awful. For years it had been quite forgotten, but now
it came back to her, how, long long ago, when she'd been a very
little girl, before Daddy had left home, she'd sometimes had this
very same feeling about him, only of course then she'd had no

power to analyse it. Mummy, somehow, had been at the back of it then: and now—in sudden fury, she knew this for absolute certain—now it was Rita! The moment she'd got home this evening—to her mother's bewilderment—she's rushed up to the bathroom and doused her pretty, floating, newly-washed hair under gallons and gallons of cold water, and then dried it in the old, bad way, in front of the electric fire, leaning so close that she almost scorched her scalp. By the time she came down to supper, it was pretty no longer, just the familiar old rats' tails, but at least Rita had been washed out of it for good. As to the nail-polish, there was no need to do anything; it had been so smudged and messed about during the commotion caused by Daddy's dramatic entrance that there was nothing left to be removed.

"No, we didn't do anything much," she answered her mother. "I just read, and did my homework. I've still got some left, actually. Quite a lot."

"You managed to find out the history questions, did you, when you went to Daphne's this morning?" Peggy enquired conversationally—and then, suddenly reminded, she abruptly interrupted herself: "Oh, and Amelia, how *did* you contrive not to see the message I left you? The message from Daddy, I mean, saying to wait here for him this afternoon, and he'd pick you up? He was furious when he found you weren't here, he thought I'd forgotten to give you the message. But I hadn't; I'd written it down specially, in huge black writing, and left it propped against the telephone when I went over to Granny's. I don't know *how* you could have missed it."

Amelia didn't know either; but she was glad of the change of subject, even though it was taking the form of a scolding.

"I suppose I was in rather a rush," she apologised vaguely; but already a little smile was beginning to play around her lips at the recollection.

For she hadn't been in a rush at all, actually. She'd been in a trance of rapture. For at Daphne's she'd learned not only what she'd gone to find out—the history questions set for the weekend's homework—but also a piece of wonderful incredible news, almost like something out of a fairy tale. Early next term—round about the middle of May—Mr Owen was to take a school party to visit

Keats's house in Hampstead. The list would be going round, Daphne had heard, this very next Monday, for people to put their names down if they wanted to go. . . .

Amelia had walked home in a daze of ecstasy, nine-tenths of her being already posed romantically underneath the mulberry tree in front of Keats's house, with Mr Owen improbably allowing the whole party to be kept waiting while Amelia Summers recited the Ode to the Nightingale, word perfect, from beginning to end.

"Woonderful!" he would murmur, his deep north-country voice tremulous with admiration; and as she stood, her eyes modestly downcast to receive her applause, a few petals of the pink blossom would float down and settle on her shoulders and her hair. Somewhere on the Heath, a cuckoo would be calling. . . .

It was little wonder that no mere telephone message, however urgent, had been able to make any sort of a dent in these visions.

"I'm sorry, Mummy, I suppose I ought to have looked," said Amelia absently; and gathering up her belongings, she drifted upstairs to finish her homework.

"Finish", actually, was something of a euphemism. As a result of all the upheavals of the afternoon, there was almost all of it still to do. Dumping her school bag on the bed, Amelia proceeded to extract from it the books she would need.

Groundwork of British History, and the file of notes that went with it. *Chambers' Second Year Algebra*. North and Hillard's *Latin Prose Composition* . . . and it was only now, with the bag almost half empty, that Amelia suddenly became aware, with a horrible lurching of the stomach, that something was missing.

Her diary! Her own private, utterly secret diary! It was gone!

Once, twice, she scrabbled frantically through the remaining books and papers. In desperation, she tipped the whole thing upside down on her bed, biscuit-crumbs and all, and searched the pile over and over again, throwing exercise-books to left and right in her growing panic.

It *must* be here! It *must*!

But it wasn't. Trying desperately to control the blind horror that was rising within her, Amelia paused and forced herself to think, quietly and objectively, of what could possibly have happened.

That the diary had been in her bag with the rest of her books when she left home, she had not the smallest doubt. She carried it with her everywhere, partly for safety's sake, and partly because she never knew when some gem of thought worthy of immortality might not strike her. And today in particular, she remembered carefully checking that it was in the bag, because there was all this wonderful news to write in it about the outing with Mr Owen, and all the afternoon at her father's in which to concentrate on it. Or so she had confidently expected; but of course, the way things had turned out, with all the unwonted alarms and disruptions, she hadn't had a minute even to think about it.

So what *had* happened? With fearful concentration, Amelia tried to reconstruct the events of the afternoon since she'd first arrived at the flat to find her father not there.

She'd dumped her school bag on the floor, unopened, she was sure of that. It had been there at her side all the time she'd been having that unsatisfactory conversation with Rita. And then—yes, that was what had happened next—she'd rushed down to Dorothy's without giving it another thought, leaving it where it lay.

And then...? And then...? After talking to Dorothy for a while, she'd come up from the basement as far as the entrance hall ... she'd encountered Kathy and the baby on the front steps, had chatted for a minute or two, and then had hung around in the street, watching for Daddy's car. After a while, she'd given it up, and had gone back upstairs to the flat, and straightaway the hair-washing business had started, and the nail-varnishing—in the midst of which Daddy had burst in, all hell had broken loose, and certainly—*certainly*—from then on, there hadn't been a moment when she could even have *thought* of unpacking her homework.

The school bag, then, had been standing untouched and unopened the entire afternoon, and, still unopened, she had picked it up at the end of her visit and taken it home.

The diary *couldn't* be gone.

The diary *was* gone.

And now, at long last, a slow and terrible comprehension began to take shape in her mind.

She sat on the edge of her bed absolutely frozen, unable to move.

CHAPTER XIV

"BUT, RITA, IT'S all just a load of nonsense! You aren't actually taking it *seriously*, are you? You can't be!"

While he spoke, Adrian was rapidly scanning the black, untidy scrawl that Rita had thrust in front of his eyes. It had obviously been written at top speed, without pause for consideration, judgement, or even legibility.

As soon as the bell went [he read] I saw Mr Owen coming out of the staff-room entrance, and he walked straight towards me across the playground. "May I carry your books, Amelia?" he asked softly, in that deep, wonderful voice of his; and together we passed through the school gates and strolled down in the direction of the river. How the other girls stared! I smiled at them, and gave Daphne a little wave, but Mr Owen had no eyes for anyone but me.

The willows were green with the first green of spring, and on the river the swans glided, keeping pace with us as we strolled along, as though they, too, would have liked to share our love, coming as close to it as they dared.

"As the swan in the evening moves over the lake ..." quoted Mr Owen in a low, throbbing voice, and I felt the vibrations of it all through me, like a thousand violins.

"Shall we sit down?" he said presently; and there, under the budding willows, he put his arm round me and bent to give me my very first kiss.

Oh, how can I describe it? What words are there in the whole of the English language. . . ?

None, apparently, because in the very next sentence (Adrian noted) the kiss is already safely over, and the couple are lying down, side by side, in the deep grass:

His arm came round me in a grip of passion, it was so strong

91

and yet so gentle . . . I thought I would die of happiness, right there in the spring sunshine.

"I love you, Amelia," he murmured, in that wonderful deep voice of his, "I've loved you ever since I first saw you, sitting in that second desk of the third row . . . but I could do nothing . . . I dared not speak. But now that my wife has left me for Another, and you and I are at last together, far beyond the imprisoning school walls, may I ask you . . . may I hope. . .?"

What Mr Owen was to be permitted to ask or to hope must for ever remain unknown, for a great smear of ink intervened here as if the book had been slammed shut in a hurry; and when the text became legible again, the happy pair are in a forest, at nightfall, and Mr Owen (with a resourcefulness surely unusual in the average I.L.E.A. employee?) is building a little hut from twigs and grass, roofed with interwoven branches, and inside Amelia is preparing a bed of leaves and moss on which (presumably) the two of them are to spend the night. Mr Owen has lit a camp-fire, too—"The smoke of it went coiling to the topmost trees"—and here they roasted beech-huts and crab-apples and recited to one another all the poems that Amelia knew by heart, pages and pages of them, including the whole of the "Ancient Mariner" as far as the bit where the Two Voices come in, and it gets boring. In the course of this recital (and no wonder, reflected Adrian, flicking over the pages with his fore-finger) night fell and the stars came out. Mr Owen's arm came round Amelia yet again, and he gave her another of those kisses for which there are no words. They roasted yet more beech-nuts, recited yet more poetry, fetched more sticks from the darkling forest, and Mr Owen's powerful features shone like gold in the light of the flickering flames. They did everything, in fact, except actually go inside that hut where the bed of moss and leaves awaited them—and then all at once, at the turning-over of a page, and without any warning at all, it is already morning, and here they are catching fish for breakfast at a crystal stream while the first rays of the rising sun strike through the trees. . . .

At this point, Adrian actually laughed aloud. Rita snatched the book from his hands, scowling.

"So it's *funny*, is it?" she demanded. "Funny-ha-ha, I suppose? Well, funny-*peculiar* is what *I'd* call it! Very peculiar indeed—for a married man in a responsible job, and the child only thirteen! I wonder if the headmistress would find it quite so funny if you were to show her—"

Adrian laughed again.

"My *dear* Rita! Don't be so idiotic! No headmistress in her senses would give a second look at such stuff! Can't you see it's fantasy from beginning to end? Well—not quite from the beginning —these first pages are dear old reality all right, I'd know it anywhere! Listen—"

Mr Owen has not marked our homework yet, so I *still* don't know if my essay will be one of the ones he reads aloud. I shan't know till *Monday*!!! Oh, doom, doom! How can I *live* through the whole weekend....

That has the unmistakable ring of truth, wouldn't you say? Or how about this?—

Mr Owen walked past the netball courts this afternoon, and I missed a goal trying to see whether he was watching me or not. Alas he wasn't; or perhaps on second thoughts *not* alas, since I made such a very boss-shot. I'd like to get marvellous at netball, so that the next time he will stop, and watch me shoot a super goal.

  Resolution: I'm not going to miss any more netball practises ever again, not even when it's Miss Dodds taking them.

                                  Signed,
                                  Amelia J. Summers.

"See what I mean?" Adrian's eyes lingered smilingly on the pain-staking little non-event recorded for all posterity in his daughter's slapdash hand. "Don't you see what's happened, Rita? The poor kid got sick of all this "Mr Owen wasn't ..." "Mr Owen didn't ..." sort of stuff, and thought she'd see if she couldn't improve on it a bit. Can you blame her?"

He smiled again, caressingly, as he re-read the passage; and when Rita remained ominously silent, he continued:

"Honestly, darling, kids *do* this sort of thing! It's nothing to get worked up about!"

At this, Rita's whole body grew tense and taut, as if preparing

93

for a spring. She whipped the volume from Adrian's hand and flicked forward through the pages with the confidence of one to whom the contents were thoroughly familiar.

"Listen to this!" she said, between clenched teeth:

His arms tightened about me, and the poppies were great scarlet moons above us. Ecstasies beyond words throbbed between us, and our souls drank the nectar of the Gods.

"Well, Daddy-dear, doesn't *that* make you wonder whether your innocent little virgin-child may not know just a teeny bit more about the details than she should?"

"Well, of course she knows! They all do, these days. She reads novels, magazine articles. For all I know, she may have read the whole of Havelock Ellis, and Alex Comfort into the bargain. And in any case, they have these sex talks and stuff at school from the age of nine or thereabouts; she'd have to be a moron not to know most of the facts by now. But, Rita, no matter how many facts she may know, *this*—here"—he jabbed at the page with his thumb— "*this* is nevertheless fantasy. Well, look at it! Use your sense. Look at what she's actually written! All this strolling down towards the river, for a start. Hasn't it occurred to you that there isn't a river within miles of the school, let alone one with swans on it? And then all this about the poppies: see the date? March 12th! When have you ever seen poppies flowering in March?"

"When have you ever seen poppies flowering in March!" mimicked Rita. "Darling, you sound just exactly like Derek! I might have guessed you'd be more interested in the time of year poppies come out than in whether your daughter is a whore or not...! All right, Adrian, laugh if you like, but it's my opinion that the whole thing should be reported to the headmistress immediately, if only for the sake of the other girls who have anything to do with this Mr Owen! I think you should ring her up straightaway tomorrow morning and tell her that..."

"Oh, Rita, don't be so utterly absurd! She'd think I was nuts! Don't you realise that kids with crushes on their English teachers are two a penny, and if the schools were to be expected to take action about every daft symptom of these adolescent passions, they'd have no time left for teaching! Here, give the thing to me, and I'll put it away safely for her till she next comes. We should never have looked at it really, not either of us; but I suppose there's no harm done so long as she never finds out. . . ."

He pulled open a drawer of his desk and, quite unaware of Rita's eyes following his every movement, he pushed the volume out of sight under a yellow folder of press-cuttings.

"There!" he said, slamming the drawer shut. "Now let's stop worrying about it and go to bed. I've had just about enough of today myself, and I should think you have too."

Adrian lay awake for a long time that night, feeling Rita's soft body nestled up against him like a small child begging to be forgiven. Although he could not bring himself to make love to her, or to feel any of that protective tenderness which usually follows a quarrel and a reconciliation, he was intensely aware of her, his brain prickly with a sort of uneasy pity. And as he lay there, restless and wakeful, he became aware not merely of a lack of tenderness, but of a growing sense of actual physical revulsion against this slender, fine-boned body which had once given him such delight.

He was appalled at the feeling. It was unjust as well as heartless. After all, he didn't *know* that those horrid anecdotes he'd been hearing about her over the weekend were true—indeed, there was substantial reason to suppose that they were not—or at least that they were greatly exaggerated. Rita herself had in effect denied them; had pointed out, very plausibly, that Derek had plenty of motive for both conscious and unconscious distortion of the truth. And as for Rita's mother, well, it was the commonest thing in the world for a grown-up daughter and her mother to be at loggerheads. The daughter is liable to be bossy and inconsiderate; and the mother, her erstwhile power gone for ever, retaliates by fishing up grievances out of the past which the daughter cannot refute because her memory does not go back that far. No doubt, Rita *had* been a horrid little girl, and a troublesome and ungrateful teenager; but the shocking and lurid anecdotes currently retailed by Mrs Fayers were doubtless exaggerated out of all recognition, having gathered to themselves over the years new and ever more colourful accretions of wickedness every time the adult Rita seriously annoyed or upset her mother: "the mother-daughter thing", as Rita herself would doubtless have labelled it. Looking back over the weekend, Adrian felt quite ashamed at having allowed his judgement to be swayed

95

by such a jumble of tittle-tattle and hearsay evidence. In the morning, he would admit this to Rita, and tell her he was sorry.

How hot it was, though, how unbearably hot! He'd never get to sleep like this. He longed to move over to his own side of the bed, to turn over and lie with his back to her on the cool, unrumpled part of the sheet. But he dared not do so for fear of waking and upsetting her. Her limp, sleeping body felt sticky in his arms, and alien somehow, almost as if it wasn't mammalian at all; a bird, perhaps, a great sticky bird, or even a vegetable—one of those exotic, tropical plants they'd seen at Kew the other day, all spines and dark fleshy leaves, mysteriously thriving in the artificial, steamy heat of the great hot-house. . . .

And a few minutes later, despite the heat, and the discomfort, and the cramp in his left arm, Adrian was asleep.

Not soundly asleep, though. His rest was broken by uneasy dreams . . . Rita, with her beautifully-manicured fingers, counting off numbers on some white-and-chrome machine of whose purpose, in the dream, he had no idea.

"Ten," he heard her clear, purposeful voice enunciating. "Ten . . . nine . . . eight . . . seven . . ." Although there seemed to be no change in the cool, dispassionate tones as the digits crept downwards, Adrian felt the beginnings of nightmare steal over him . . . and he knew that *something* . . . something terrible . . . was just about to happen. But before it happened he was somehow already in another dream, not a terrible one at all this time, not in its beginnings, though perhaps with a slight sense of anxiety about it. He dreamed that it was evening, and that he had come home to the flat carrying in his briefcase some piece of work which was very much on his mind—an emergency report to look over, something like that. There was some piece of information urgently needed for the work —some fact or date that he had to look up—and he walked in his dream over to the bookshelves and pulled out a volume of the *Encyclopaedia Britannica*. It seemed heavier than he remembered, and as he braced his muscles against the unexpected weight, he was aware once again of the onset of nightmare. With a sort of dreadful inevitability, the volume fell open, and there, squashed between the pages, like a book-marker, like a pressed flower for remembrance, lay the budgerigar: dead, pressed out flat to three or four times its natural size, its blood-stained feathers partially plucked and oozing on to the page.

"I thought I'd mark the place for you, darling," said the dream-Rita, smiling down at him, with an air of intelligent interest in his work which she had never shown in life; "I thought that if I—"

Adrian awoke, certain that he was screaming at the very top of his lungs, rousing the whole house. But of course he wasn't: only the very tiniest little catch in his breath marked his awakening, and his whole soul was flooded with thankfulness at the realisation that the whole ghastly experience was at an end.

Or was it? He lay there, sweating and panting, trying to recover from the dream as one recovers from a sudden attack of illness. Even now, wide awake and fully conscious, the feel of Rita's soft skin pressed against his own made his flesh crawl. He was aware, with his rational mind, of how utterly unfair to her this was; but there was nothing he could do about it.

He slept no more that night. Presently, the darkness gave way to the grey light of dawn; and by the time the first pink of sunrise filtered through the curtains, he knew what he had to do.

Knew, too, though helpless as a zombie to prevent it, how cruel and unfair he was being.

CHAPTER XV

RITA WAS TAKING it quite extraordinarily well: no tears, no scenes, no recriminations. In fact, she spoke hardly at all. She just sat quietly on the edge of the bed, shoulders hunched a little as though against a shower of rain, and allowed the clichés to pour over her.

"Nobody's fault . . ." "neither of us really to blame . . ." "just one of those things . . ." "better now than later . . ." "will always treasure the good times we had together . . ."—and only when Adrian had quite run out of these stock phrases and manufactured sentiments did Rita look up at him, and enquire meekly, like an au-pair girl who has failed to give satisfaction, how soon he wanted her to go?

The guilt was awful. Adrian did not know what to say or where to look. He had been counting, he realised now, on a blazing row, a scene of savage mutual recrimination to oil the wheels of parting. Faced instead by acquiescence on this monstrous and wholly unprecedented scale, he simply did not know what to do next. All the tortured resolutions of the night seemed to be crumbling beneath the weight of Rita's non-resistance, leaving him bereft of motivation. He stared at her helplessly, as if waiting for her instructions; but her meekness seemed impregnable, she turned the other cheek relentlessly, like some sort of battering-ram.

"This morning, did you mean?" she persisted humbly. "Did you want me to pack up and go right now? I could, if you like"—and by the time Adrian had expressed his outrage at this suggestion, and had assured her that he'd never meant to hurry her in the very least, that of course she must take her time, make plans at leisure, and that the last thing he wanted to do was to put any pressure on her—by his time it was quite unclear, even to Adrian, whether he was persuading her to go or to stay. With a wild, unseeing glance at his watch, and a meaningless mutter of sheer desperation, he made a dive for the bathroom, slammed and bolted the door, and turned on all the taps to their fullest extent, as if to drown under the gushing water the tumult of his indecision.

There was no tumult really; and certainly not one of indecision. The decision had been made during the night; and it had been a right one. The harsh clarity of that sleepless dawn had shown him things about himself, and about his relationship with Rita, which he had not wanted to face; but they were true things. Lying now in the hot, enveloping water, Adrian realised that though Rita's response to his ultimatum had startled him almost out of his senses, it hadn't, in fact, changed anything, or modified in the very least degree any of the factors which had made him resolve to break with her.

"Factors"? There was only one factor really, and Adrian thought about it, sadly, while slowly and luxuriously soaping himself. It was difficult, now, to remember exactly when it was that he had stopped loving Rita, because he had refused to admit it, even to himself, for such a very long time. It is pleasanter to be in love than not to be; and to think that you are is at least better than nothing. And so the weeks and months had gone by, and he hadn't wanted to notice that there was any change, and anyway, it had all been so very gradual. The whole thing, of course, had been brought to a head by this foolhardy attempt to live together. Many a good love affair has foundered on this rock, and Rita must surely have been aware of the risk she was taking in moving in on him the way she did. Admittedly, he'd sometimes asked her to do just this, and had told her how enchanting he would find it; but surely a grown woman, past thirty, should have known better than to put faith in vague protestations of devotion? Surely a lover is *entitled* to tell a certain number of lies, some of the time? It simply isn't *fair* to believe every word a man says. . . .

But hardly had this comfortably self-justifying thought taken shape in Adrian's brain than another, even better, one followed hot on its heels, and with an exultant swirl of water around shoulders and knees, he allowed it to take possession of his mind.

What a fool he'd been! What a blind, conceited idiot! Why hadn't it occurred to him before that all the time he'd been reluctantly falling out of love with Rita, *she* had probably been falling out of love with him likewise? And meanwhile both of them, out of the usual mixture of cowardice, vanity and sentimentality, had been refusing to admit it.

The more Adrian reflected on this new possibility, the more he approved of it. It explained everything, which satisfied his scientific temperament, and it also released him from all further guilt and heart-searching. All that farrago of apologies and explanations that he'd spent half the night concocting, in a sweat of compunction and guilt—it had all been unnecessary! Rita hadn't minded! *That's* why she hadn't cried and stormed and made a scene—it was because she hadn't minded!

How simple things can be! Adrian felt that there was a moral in this somewhere, but before he'd had time to work it out, his attention was caught by the "ping" of the telephone being replaced. He hadn't heard Rita's voice at all—the sitting-room door must have been shut as well as the bathroom one—and he wondered, vaguely, who she could have been ringing so early in the morning. But he quickly decided that, whoever it was, it was a Good Thing. It meant that she was taking action—making plans of one sort or another. Arranging to go and stay with her mother, maybe? Or even with Derek? Not that this last seemed at all likely, in the circumstances; but anyway, she was phoning *somebody*, that was the main thing. With a vague sense of accomplishment, of having brought things to a satisfactory conclusion, Adrian lurched upwards from the cooling water and reached for a towel.

Far away across London, Amelia laid down the receiver, and stood staring at it, as if she still could not believe what she had heard.

And indeed she could not. The thing was so monstrous, so unspeakably appalling, that she simply could not take it in. At first, she had not even recognised Rita's voice, so soft was it, and so carefully pitched; and when, after some seconds, she did begin to recognise it, she still could not believe what she was hearing.

She'd thought, at first, that it must be some obscene kind of a joke. That Rita had discovered her precious and most private diary—this she gathered quite early on; that Rita had read it, too, and been "disgusted" by it—this, also, she managed to take in, bewildered, and speechless with fury. But when Rita went on to inform her, softly, and in dead earnest, that she intended to take the diary up to the school this very day and show it to the headmistress—"and *then* what will happen to your precious Mr Owen?"—at this point, Amelia's thought processes simply blacked out: the horror of the thing was beyond what her mind could grasp. She simply stood there, unable to move or speak, while Rita's low, careful voice purred on and on, and finally came to a stop; and even then, with the dead phone buzzing on and on in her ear, she still went on standing there. No one interrupted her, or broke into her trance of horror, for Peggy had already just left for work when the call came. Rita had timed it well; and even if Amelia had retained the presence of mind to try and ring her father, she would not have been able to get through. Rita had the thing well in hand; she had been planning it since quite early this morning.

And so the minutes ticked by, until presently half an hour had passed. Already, Amelia was late for school. She couldn't go, of course, she could never go again, she would stay at home and kill herself, but even that wouldn't do any good, because it wouldn't stop Mr Owen seeing the awful things she'd written, wouldn't stop him being shocked and revolted . . . merely being dead is no protection against this sort of thing.

Might there, though, be some way of averting the catastrophe? Amelia's numbed mind was beginning, a little bit at a time, to function again, and she set herself to devising desperate measures of counter-attack. Like capturing Rita, and tying her up somewhere? Or waylaying her outside the school, and taking the diary by force, knocking her down in the street if necessary?

But outside which entrance should Amelia lie in wait? While she hovered near the staff-room steps, Rita could be slipping down through the Middle School basement cloakroom; while Amelia mounted guard by the main entrance, Rita could be gaining admittance through the porter's lodge—oh, there were a dozen ways! And besides, how could Amelia hope to hang about unnoticed for any length of time? "Pst! Amelia! I say, Amelia, Music's started! Miss Lucas'll be *furious*!" or, "Amelia Summers! May I enquire what you think you're doing out here in the street during school hours. . .?" Oh, it would be hopeless! Worse than hopeless, for it would call everyone's attention to her before she'd had any chance to do anything.

Of course, if she'd only known when Rita intended to go, it would have been easier; but naturally Rita hadn't given her any inkling at all, she was far too cunning. At some unknown hour, from some unknown direction, Rita was going to slip along by some unpredictable route, and gain admission to the school. It was all planned, specially, evilly planned, so that Amelia should have all the agony of knowing what was about to happen, and yet no opportunity of averting it.

There was no way. No way at all.

"I'll kill her!" screamed Amelia into the empty house. "I will! I'll kill her! KILL her, KILL her, KILL her!"

And that evening, just after six, news came from the school that Rita had been found lying at the foot of the Art Room stairs with her neck broken.

CHAPTER XVI

THIS, AT LEAST, was the substance of the story brought by Daphne, arriving hot-foot from the scene of the disaster. Or if not precisely the scene itself, at least straight from the thrilling presence of a girl whose sister's best friend actually *had* been there, right on the spot. Well, practically on the spot: she'd heard the screams, anyway, and had watched the ambulance driving away.

It had happened like this. This girl, Rosemary Something, a Fifth-Former, had chanced to be staying on after school for a final rehearsal of the Upper School play; and just as the final tragic scene was coming up, with the chorus of Greek women all tearing their hair and bewailing their destiny almost without a slip—just at this juncture, there'd been these awful screams. It was hard to tell just where they were coming from; in the deserted school building everything echoed so, up and down the empty stairs and corridors. Anyway, they'd all rushed along, pell mell, just as they were, clutching at their safety-pinned Grecian robes, head-dresses and myrtle wreaths all awry, but by the time they'd located the scene of the accident, most of the excitement was already over. A little knot of cleaners, and a teacher or two, were still gathered by the front entrance, watching the departing ambulance; and from the buzz of excited talk Rosemary gleaned what titbits of information she could with which to regale her family at the tea-table; from which, in turn, her young sister collected random earfuls to share with such friends and class-mates as lived nearby. And so now here was Daphne, hopping from one leg to another with impatience, and well-nigh collapsing under her surfeit of undivulged news.

But Peggy was adamant. Amelia was very much upset, she said primly, and wouldn't want to see anyone just now. She did not feel it necessary to add that none of this had anything to do with Rita's accident; that Amelia did not even know about it yet, and whatever was the cause of her distress it could not be *that*, as it had been going on all day, long before Rita had so much as set foot on those fateful stairs.

This, at least, was how Peggy read the situation. She had come home from work to find her daughter already quite worn out with grief and despair, her face so swollen with crying as to be hardly recognisable. Nothing Peggy could do—no persuasions, no loving cajolery, not even a sharp, last-resort scolding—would induce her to say one single word in explanation.

"Leave me *alone*" was the only response Peggy could extract from her. "*Please*, Mummy, just leave me alone!" She would eat no tea, would listen to no endearments; just lay on her bed in silent misery, occasionally making a low moaning noise, like a trapped, tortured animal.

And so it seemed to Peggy, who had to make a lightning door-step decision on the question, that to let Daphne in with her alarming and shocking news about Rita could only do harm. Amelia just wouldn't be able to take it.

Not that Peggy had any idea of how Amelia would react to the shock. A little while ago—only a few days ago, in fact—she would have said that Amelia was really growing quite fond of this woman who had become for all practical purposes her stepmother; but now she was not so sure. It was very hard to tell, one way or the other, because Amelia had taken to being so very reticent about these Sunday afternoon visits. She hardly ever told her mother anything at all about what had happened, and only very occasionally did she inadvertently drop some clue as to how she was feeling: which wasn't much to go on, really. Most of the time, Peggy felt wholly in the dark.

At the beginning, Peggy had worried a lot about the situation, fearing, as did Adrian, that the child would be miserably jealous and resentful of this newcomer's intrusion into her father's life, and the happy Sunday visits would be spoiled for ever. Peggy was not the sort of ex-wife who rejoices gleefully over every setback in the relationship of her child and her ex-husband; on the contrary, she liked the people around her to be happy, ex-husbands and all. Whether this was due to any exceptional saintliness in her nature, or simply to the fact that she had discovered that happy people are on the whole less trouble than unhappy ones, she would have found it hard to decide.

Above all, of course, she liked her daughter to be happy, and this was why—quite apart from the natural hurt to herself—she had been so perturbed by the recent changes in Amelia's behaviour

—particularly on Sunday evenings. Sulky—off-hand—almost rude: surely it meant that something must be wrong? Especially since the two of them had always been so close until now, and had had such fun together. Peggy had been worrying about it lately quite a bit, and had hoped, secretly, that her friends—particularly Maureen Denvers—hadn't noticed the deterioration of the mother-daughter relationship. Having a "good relationship" with your children rated very high in Peggy's circle—much higher, for instance, than expensive cars or exotic holidays—and of course, if you had a broken marriage to carry about with you everywhere (because this was what it felt like, Peggy found; you could never leave it behind and forget about it)—well, then, in that case your "good relationship" had to be better than good, it had to be visibly marvellous, for it was going to be subjected to much severer scrutiny than were all those ramshackle, bickering two-parent set-ups that managed to get by simply because they *were* two-parent. A married pair can get away with having a much unhappier, more neurotic child than can any single parent; it had often struck Peggy as rather unfair that this should be so, though until recently it hadn't actually affected her personally. Amelia had up till now been a singularly satisfactory daughter to have—happy, clever, well-mannered, and a wonderful companion. It was only just lately that things had begun to go wrong; and even then Peggy had quite often been inclined to put it all down to adolescence, and to the psychological upheavals that one had been vaguely led to expect at such a time.

But not today; today something really *was* the matter, something terrible; and in the face of this certainty, all the psychological theories collapsed like a house of cards. They became quite useless, it seemed, as soon as something *actually* went wrong, with your own *actual* child.

And now, on top of all this, there was Rita's accident! Why must the idiot woman choose today of all days for falling over her crazy built-up heels, or whatever it was she'd done? And what was Peggy supposed to do about it, anyway? What *is* the rôle of the ex-wife when the current mistress is lying at death's door? The etiquette books haven't caught up with this sort of thing yet, so Peggy had no guidance; but an uneasy instinct warned her that it was her duty to do *something*. She'd already phoned Adrian, phoned Derek, and phoned the school, but they'd all been line-engaged. Now she phoned them again, still with no result; and really, there seemed nothing further she could do. She didn't even know if Rita was alive or dead, and it didn't seem necessary, just yet, to examine her heart and see whether she cared; time enough for that when she knew whether it had happened.

It was too much! Too much happening all at once. Filled with a sense of vague, all-embracing dread, Peggy tiptoed back into Amelia's room, half expecting, like the nervous mother of a new-born baby, to find that she had stopped breathing.

She hadn't, of course. If anything, she was breathing more normally than before, and with less of a sob in her throat. Also, Esben was curled up on the end of the bed this time—always a good sign, because Esben, like most cats, hated people to be crying and writhing about, disturbing all the nice warm surfaces.

The room was growing dark now, and looking down at the tear-sodden lump of doom under the eiderdown, unresponsive as a length of board, Peggy experienced, quite without warning, a sudden uprush of irritation. What right had the girl to cause all this anxiety, to frighten everybody out of their wits without volunteering a single word of explanation? And particularly at a time like this, when a *real* disaster had just struck, demanding everyone's attention and concern. And then, with compunction, Peggy recollected that as yet Amelia knew nothing about the accident: indeed, it was Peggy herself who was deliberately keeping it from her, and so it was hardly fair to blame the child for not taking it into consideration . . . and just at that moment, the telephone shrilled through the house.

"Adrian? Oh, thank goodness it's you . . . I've been trying and trying to ring you. Oh, my dear, I'm *so sorry* . . . so terribly, terribly sorry! Is she . . . ? I mean, have you heard yet. . . .?"

Disgruntled, and somehow a little bit scared by her reception, Daphne turned slowly away from the uncompromisingly closed front door, and retraced her steps.

What a pig Mrs Summers was! *Of course* Amelia would have wanted to see her! Even if she *was* as much upset by her step-mother's accident as Mrs Summers implied—and Daphne, for one, was sceptical about it—even so, she'd still have wanted to talk about it to her friends, especially a best friend like Daphne. Anyone

would. Whatever happened to you, however frightful, you always
wanted to talk about it to your *friends*, it was the very first thing
you did want to do. If Amelia really *was* upset, then she'd be
wanting more than anything to talk to Daphne. It was *mean* of
Mrs Summers, really it was.

Besides—and this was what was really gnawing away at Daphne's
innermost soul—besides, everyone would be *expecting* her to have
talked to Amelia Summers! They were best friends, weren't they?
At break tomorrow, she, Daphne, would be bombarded with questions which it would be an awful come-down not to be able to
answer. Was it true that the victim's neck was *broken*? Flopping
about on her shoulders do you mean—like *this*? Was she going to
die? To be paralysed for life? Was her brain affected? Could she
still speak? Or was she going to be like those people from the
Home who came into the High Street in wheelchairs on
Saturdays?

How glorious if Daphne could have been the one with all the
answers at her finger-tips! The one who could describe all the
gruesome details! And to think that only the arbitrary maternal
whims of the wretched Mrs Summers had stood between her and
this once-in-a-lifetime glory!

Honestly, *mothers*!

Actually, Daphne had been setting her hopes altogether too high,
right from the beginning. Amelia or no Amelia, she wouldn't have
been able to answer her schoolmates' questions because no one
could. Even the chief surgeon at the hospital couldn't have answered
them. Not, that is, until the X-ray results had come through, and
Rita herself had come out of her state of shock sufficiently to be
asked to move this group of muscles or that; to answer Yes or No
to whether she felt the prick of a pin here . . . or here?

But the prognosis, at the end of forty-eight hours, was good. Her
spine had not, after all, been fractured. There were some cracked
vertebrae and a cervical dislocation, which would necessitate the
wearing of a spinal jacket and a neck-brace for the next few weeks,
but there was every reason to suppose that she would thereafter
be completely recovered. And meantime, there was no reason,
barring some unforeseeable setback, why she should not leave
hospital within the next week or so.

The good news was relayed round family and friends in a matter of minutes. There were congratulations, get-well cards, flowers. And it so happened that Amelia's friend Daphne did, after all, get her moment of glory, albeit belatedly. For as it chanced, the affair got a brief mention in the local press on the following Friday, and Daphne it was who spotted the item and brought the cutting gleefully to school, to pass round, with furtive gasps and whisperings, during the history lesson. It was a good report of its kind, concise and factual, the reporter allowing himself only one brief bit of fashionable moralising about "authorities" who permit the erection of staircases that can be fallen down. The fact that any staircase which can't be fallen down also can't be walked down, could be glossed over as an example of "officialdom at its worst". After all, *someone* must be to blame for gravitation, and if it isn't the I.L.E.A., then what are we paying all these taxes for?

Or words to that effect. Anyway, having dutifully pointed the moral which would best please most of his readers the writer returned to the hard facts, including some hastily-assembled data about Rita, and a smudged but unmistakably glamorous picture of her nestled among her bandages, her black hair loose and splayed out over a lacy bed-jacket.

"Someone pushed me" was the arresting caption to this photograph; but in the copy below she was quoted as having added warily, "but I'm naming no names!"

"It is expected that the police will be following up these allegations," the reporter surmised cautiously; and having thus squeezed the last drop of news-value from the thing, he brought his account briskly to an end.

The girls loved it. It passed swiftly and furtively back and forth under the desks, until the running commentary of whispers and giggles finally reached a pitch which Mr Everard could no longer ignore. Laying down chalk and duster with a sigh, he confiscated the thing, and with a few sharp words, and a couple of detentions, brought the class back to a proper concern for Disraeli's speeches about the Corn Laws. One girl, who just couldn't stop giggling, he sent outside, and two others were quelled by a shaft of well-timed sarcasm.

And to Daphne belonged the honour and glory of having started the whole thing! She got a special telling off all to herself, and when she went out to break found she had become the unquestioned authority on plaster jackets, stepmothers, slipped discs, paralysis, and brain tumours. It was wonderful.

Poor Amelia! This should have been her show really, thought Daphne pityingly; but then, she should never have been absent during such a week! She, Daphne, would have had herself brought to school on a *stretcher* before she'd have missed it all.

CHAPTER XVII

NOTHING IS MORE unpredictable than the kind of invalid a person will make. Selfish, demanding egotists in ordinary life can become angels of patience and humble gratitude under the on-slaught of pain: life-long paragons of self-denial and concern for others can become monsters of peevish ill-nature at the first lash of illness.

Adrian was dreading Rita's return from hospital, though he was less scared, actually, about what sort of a patient *she* would make than about what sort of a ministering angel *he* would. At the best of times, he disliked illness, and shrank from its manifestations, in himself or others. He had always observed, with a sort of incredulous wonder, the extraordinary demands human beings allow illness to make on them, the sufferer no less than his attendants. Whereas in every other known mammalian species, the sick individual crawls off into a dark corner by itself to recover in solitude, the human mammal imposes the exact opposite on its sick members, setting them up into a position of glaring prominence, and floodlighting them with a multi-faceted concern from which there is no way of hiding. Propped up amid flowers, grapes and get-well cards, like an emperor among his jewels, the victim becomes, despite his weakness, a nerve-centre of comings and goings, a focal point of elaborate and inescapable ceremonial. Enthroned among his pillows, bound by a ritual as rigid as that of any mediaeval court, he is expected to receive state visits from all and sundry, to give audience at appointed hours to deputations from here, there and everywhere, and to sustain these encounters smilingly, with un-faltering aplomb, like royalty. In all this he is expected to play the lead, to keep his end up, to observe the elaborate protocol of greetings and farewells, and to show himself well versed in the formulae prescribed for the gracious acceptance of tribute in the form of chocolates, busy-lizzies, and comic pictures of bedpans.

All this when you are *ill*, for heaven's sake! And even this isn't the end of the story. There is a sort of monstrous arrogance about illness—anyone's illness—to which Adrian could never reconcile himself: the way it takes precedence over anything and everything, driving tank-like over all concerns other than its own. Thus by being in hospital (even though it was now clear that she was going to recover), Rita had put herself out of range of all her problems, including those she was currently causing for others. For days— maybe for weeks—no one could ask her to face up to anything, to discuss anything uncomfortable or unpleasant. Certainly, it was going to be impossible for Adrian to follow up that last conversation he'd had with her before the accident, in which it had been agreed that she was to leave him. It wasn't an agreement you could hold her to now, or even refer to any more: her accident had released her totally, for the foreseeable future, from anything she had said or promised, and from the consequences of anything she had ever done. Nothing was her fault any more; all was perforce forgiven.

It was like a sort of mini-Millenium, only with everyone else carrying the can, instead of God.

This awful power of Rita's illness crushed Adrian into the ground. He felt like a non-man, all his own projects and purposes suddenly obliterated. It was like waking up in the morning to find his whole life buried under a fall of snow, leaving only Rita's sick-bed concerns visible, sticking up like telegraph poles as far as the eye could see.

Adrian wondered whether, deep in their hearts, everyone felt like this about illness? Or was he alone in his monstrous callous-ness? If, indeed, you could call it callousness, when he was only too ready to apply to himself the same criteria as to others? In fact, he himself had never been seriously ill; but if such a thing should happen, his desire would be to be left severely alone and, apart from necessary medical treatments (applied as impersonally as possible), to be allowed to crawl away into that dark mammalian corner. That this was what he would prefer for himself, he was absolutely certain, and indeed, to be quite honest, he would prefer it for other people, too; but luckily one was never called upon to be *that* honest. The ritual took over, and with its mighty, centuries-old power quelled such opinions at their source.

Nevertheless, what with one thing and another, it did seem that Adrian was not quite the man to be landed with sick-nursing on any very extensive scale. But then, neither was Rita the woman to be landed with wearing a neck-brace for the greater part of the summer. It is a hard but inescapable fact that Fate takes no account of natural aptitude when dealing out her blows.

There was a brief moment, about three days before Rita was due to come out of hospital, when Adrian indulged a wild but short-lived vision of getting out of the thing altogether. He arrived at his office, rather later than usual, to be told by his secretary that Mr Langley had phoned twice already, and would Adrian ring him back immediately, as it was urgent?

Urgent! What glorious visions the word conjured up, of Derek indignantly demanding his rights as a husband! Insisting that his wife be sent back to *him* to convalesce! Perhaps the hospital had been on to the phone to him this morning, or he to them, to clear the matter up, and perhaps, with a sudden rush of male pride to the head, Derek had averred that over his dead body would he allow his wife, in her fragile state, to be handed over to that callous, double-dealing, sex-crazy son-of-a-bitch....

But as soon as he heard Derek's mild, unemphatic voice at the other end of the wire, he realised, with a sinking of the heart, that here was no manic upsurge of outraged masculinity to be dealt with; rather, it was the very same disability that was affecting Adrian himself; an upsurge of overwhelming desire to avoid bother, by any means within the bounds of common decency.

Rita, apparently, had rung Derek from her bedside this morn-ing, at an hour which for her, hospital-orientated as she had become, was just after breakfast, but which for him was practically the middle of the night, to suggest that she should come home to him in Wimbledon to convalesce. Perhaps being woken from his deepest sleep had been a factor contributing to Derek's attitude of unqualified disfavour towards this proposal, or maybe the dis-favour would in any case have been overwhelming; anyway, by the time Adrian was on the line to him, his attitude was crystal clear, and unshakeable.

"You see, my dear fellow," he explained equably, "you didn't, as I understand it, take her away from me on a sale-or-return basis. It was theft, you know, plain outright theft; and even in these days, when burglars have never had it so good, they still have not been accorded the legal right to return goods which are faulty, or which fail to give satisfaction. In addition to which, my dear chap, you will, I am sure, appreciate that you have left it a bit late in the day, you are no longer in what one might call a sellers' market. She's damaged goods, isn't she?—as one might say; in a manner of speaking. . . ."

Adrian retorted sharply that this was no way to talk about the poor girl and her accident, which had only just escaped being a very serious one indeed; and Derek agreed that No, indeed it wasn't, and no doubt Adrian himself had some much, much nicer things to say about it? He, Derek, was all ears.

At this, naturally, Adrian was rendered speechless. It took him several seconds to adjust to the extraordinary turn the conversation had taken, and to take in that the gist of it, so far, amounted to a quite unfounded charge against himself: an accusation of wanting to push Rita, now that she was ill, back on to Derek. This was just exactly what he did want, of course, but this was no reason for accusing him of it.

"What the hell is this all about, anyway?" he blustered, trying to capture the initiative. "When did I ever say anything about Rita's returning to you? As a matter of fact, I've assumed all along that naturally *I* shall—"

" '*Naturally*!' Dear, dear!" Derek gave a small unpleasant laugh, and then continued: "My dear chap, don't get me wrong: please don't think that I'm *objecting* to your noble, gentlemanly, and very proper reluctance to throw my wife on the scrap-heap as soon as she becomes a bit of a burden. Not a bit of it. On the contrary, I applaud such a decision. But to ask me to believe that it is *natural* in you to behave like this—that is, with common decency. . . ."

"Derek! Look, this isn't getting us anywhere—!"

Adrian felt perturbed rather than angry. These elaborate and gratuitous insults were too blatant to be taken at face value; they seemed to indicate a bitterness run out of control rather than straightforward enmity. Had something new happened? And if so, what. . . ?

"Listen," he went on, "this is no time for slanging each other and trying to sort out the rights and wrongs of the thing. I've no doubt there's plenty I should be apologising for. But right now, with Rita in hospital after a really very nasty accident . . ."

" 'Accident'? Ah yes, of course, I'd forgotten that you'd still be using that word for it. Of course you would. '*Naturally*.' But that's not what the paper said, is it? And it's not what Rita herself says. She says . . ."

Suddenly, light dawned. For a moment, Adrian was too astounded to speak. He, of course, like everyone else, had seen the quote in the paper, had been shocked by it; but then, when nothing further happened, and when Rita herself made no further reference to the matter, he concluded that the whole thing must have been a bit of journalistic kite-flying, or that Rita, if she had spoken the words at all, had spoken them while still in a state of shock, and not knowing what she was saying. The people at the hospital must, he judged, have reached the same conclusion, or else by now, surely, the police or someone would have taken some sort of action?

He began explaining all this to Derek, in the smiling, throw-away tones of a man clearing up a ridiculous little misunderstanding between friends. But the silence from Derek's end of the phone was total, and went on and on. Adrian found himself beginning to ramble uneasily, to lose the thread of what he was saying.

"I mean, hang it all, Derek," he found himself expostulating, as much to extract some sort of response from Derek's end of the line as to defend himself, "I mean, you can't be seriously suggesting that *I*—"

"Of course not!" Derek's voice sprang back into the ear-piece with a suddenness that made Adrian jump. "Of course I'm not suggesting it, I wouldn't be such a fool! It would only set you polishing up your alibi to even smoother perfection, wouldn't it? And I'm sure it's an excellent one already. I won't even waste time on checking on it, whatever it is, so certain am I that it will prove watertight. '*Naturally*' it will. But I thought you might like to know that *if* the police should take it into their heads to come and question me, then I shall feel obliged to reveal to them the fact that Rita rang me up that very morning—the morning of the day of the "accident"—and told me that you were throwing her out. She was very distressed, poor girl, she wanted to come back to *me*, to her dreary old no-good husband! Would you credit it? Maybe if I'd agreed, if I'd said, Yes, darling, you pack your things right away and come back to your own sweetie-pie who loves you —well, if I'd said *that*, then maybe the "accident" would never have happened. Would it? Because, my dear Adrian, you only had the two ways of getting rid of her, hadn't you? She's not the sort of girl to go off and stand on her own two feet, you know *that* as well as I do. She has to cling, Rita does, she's like that special dwarf variety of wisteria of mine, which was among the plants that she destroyed so effectively—it was hanging like little black bootlaces from its trellis, did you notice? Of course you did —and of course you know that that's what she is, too—a clinger. She'd never have left you until she was sure she could come back to me—you'd have had her on your back for ever. And so when I, selfish creature that I am, said Not B-Likely—*that* was the moment, wasn't it, when you realised that you now had only the one other option left to you? And so really"—here Derek's voice took on a meditative quality, as of one philisophising about Life and the Human Condition—"and so really, it was my selfishness, wasn't it, just as much as your murderous violence, that pushed her down that flight of stairs? We murdered her together, didn't we?— attempted it, that is to say.

"Butter-fingers, eh, both of us. . . ?"

CHAPTER XVIII

IN ALL HIS self-absorbed and unheroic dread of Rita's home-coming, Adrian had forgotten one vital factor: Dorothy. He should have foreseen that Dorothy was going to absolutely love it, just as she'd been absolutely loving the whole thing right from the beginning—from the first horrifying phone call, right through the paralysed-for-life scare to the startling "someone pushed me" allegations. For her, Rita's return with her back dramatically in plaster was going to be the grand finale of the most glorious catastrophe in all her years as a landlady, and she wasn't for worlds going to miss out on one single detail of any of it. And of course, in the process of not missing out, she was inevitably going to make things much, much easier for Adrian. Long ago, Dorothy had discovered that only by helping people in their troubles do you get to the real, juicy core of the disaster, in all its scandalous and thrilling details; and now, true to her lifelong philosophy, she was only too willing to help Rita—*really* to help her—spending half her days up in the flat doing with generous gusto anything that needed doing.

And of course, lots of things *did* need doing, especially during those first days of all, when Rita could only walk with extreme difficulty, stiff as an upended roll of lino, and couldn't sit down at all without assistance.

Dorothy was in her element, her kindness, her curiosity and her unquenchable delight in the horrific combining to produce just that blend of inquisitive concern and practical usefulness which is invaluable in a sick-room. She helped unstintingly, cooking, cleaning, ironing, making beds, so that when Adrian came home in the evenings there was hardly a thing left for him to do. He was absolutely thankful; it allowed him to get on with his work and all his usual activities almost as if nothing had happened.

And so it came about that it was to Dorothy, not to Adrian, that Rita first confided her fears. She felt "scared", she said, of being right up here at the top of the house. She kept fancying she heard footsteps on the stairs: strange shufflings and bumpings in the adjoining room.

Dorothy was sympathy itself. She could quite understand this feeling, she declared, so weak as Rita still was, and with that great heavy thing around her neck. It must make her feel, Dorothy surmised, dreadfully helpless "if anything was to happen".

"Just how my grandma used to feel when she had her hip."—Dorothy enlarged on the theme—"*She* was living up top of a big house at the time, too, and being used to servants and all that in her young days, you know, she couldn't get used to the idea of being up there on her own and it's being no one's job to look after her. 'Suppose there was a fire!' she used to say. 'Or robbers! How would I ever get down the stairs fast enough?' "

Dorothy's grandmother—her hip, her delicate nerves and her aristocratic forbears—kept Dorothy up in the flat ironing and tidying for an entire afternoon, and by a natural enough sequence of ideas these topics led to a reference to the old diary, including all that name-dropping of long ago. Amelia Caroline Ponsonby. One of *the* Ponsonbys.

"Amelia—*our* Amelia, that's to say—she was thrilled to bits when I let her see it," Dorothy chatted on, slowly pushing the iron back and forth over one of Adrian's shirts. "Funny thing, wasn't it, *both* of them being called 'Amelia'! And on top of that, here's *our* Amelia keeping a diary too! She was telling me all about it, how— Why, whatever's the matter, dear? Aren't you feeling well? Got a funny turn, have you? It's like that, you know, when you first come out of hospital. Very funny you can feel sometimes, all of a sudden. I remember the lady who was here—let me see—not the last one before Kathy and that lot, but the one before that— Well, she'd had this operation, you see, gall-bladder it was, dreadful pain she'd been having, and the very day she come out, she . . ."

But Rita, rigid in her plaster casing, was still trembling, her jaw shaking atop its rampart; and when Adrian came in that evening Dorothy took it upon herself to waylay him on the stairs and describe the whole episode to him, and to surmise, with grave looks and ecstatic head-shakings, that the poor thing's nerves were still not right, not right at all, and that in Dorothy's opinion she should never have . . .

Adrian leaned against the banisters, frowning impatiently. He did not at all want to snub Dorothy, especially after all her kindness—which indeed had by now become indispensable to him—but he hated having to be dragged into Rita's emotional state, being forced to consider what was, or might be, going on in her mind.

For, apart from politenesses and trivial platitudes, he and Rita had conversed hardly at all since her return from hospital, and Adrian was praying that it might go on that way. There had, it is true, been a brief spell immediately after Derek's ridiculous phone call when it had crossed Adrian's mind to have the whole thing out with Rita straightaway, at the very next visiting hour: to ask her what on earth she'd actually meant by that astounding statement to the press, and whom she was meaning to accuse? He had thought about doing this; had thought about just how to word it; and in the end had done nothing. It is always easier to do nothing than something, and in this case he could tell himself that he was putting the thing off for Rita's sake—that she was still in a shaky state, and must not be upset. In the course of these reflections he began to see the point, after all, of the irritating sanctity of illness, which he had always so deplored: it seemed that it allowed other people, as well as the patient, to procrastinate and to escape responsibilities. Of course, he told himself, there would have to be a proper confrontation *some* time, not only about Rita's mysterious accusation, but also about the question of what the hell she was doing at the school in the first place. "Amelia asked me to come"—Rita's explanation so far—just didn't make sense; and he couldn't, at the moment, check it with Amelia herself because the Easter holidays had started, and Peggy on a sudden whim had taken the child down to Seaford "for a change of air", and they wouldn't be back for a fortnight or more.

"Yes, well, thank you, Dorothy. Thanks for telling me," he kept saying, one hand on the banisters; but still Dorothy kept right on talking, until, mercifully, a diversion was created in the shape of a sullen, overweight youth, whom Adrian hadn't seen before, pushing his way wordlessly past them and out through the front door. Dorothy's ever-hungry attention was immediately caught by this new phenomenon, and the almost-talked-out subject of Rita's nerves was temporarily forgotten.

"See?" She leaned towards Adrian confidentially. "See? I believe that's Kathy's new boy friend! That's the *third* time he's been here! Oh, I do hope so, poor kid, she's had such rotten luck so far! All those hippies and layabouts—but this one, he looks a different type, didn't you think? Not good-looking of course, not like That Brian, but more sort of *steady*. Didn't you think so?"

Adrian, who had thought nothing except that his new incumbent (if such he was) seemed just as unmannerly as his predecessors, could find nothing to say. He hadn't been following Kathy's love-life with sufficient attention to have an opinion of any kind. On the other hand, he had no wish to damp down any of Dorothy's facile enthusiasms, which so often proved so beneficial to all concerned—and not least to himself at this present juncture. So he simply made an indeterminate, vaguely encouraging sound and seized the opportunity to escape.

He approached his own landing feeling unsettled and appre-hensive. Despite his boredom with the conversation, Dorothy's words had sunk in—or some of them had. He was annoyed at being made to feel anxious about Rita again just when things were beginning to be not too bad; and he began fighting back against Dorothy's unsettling insinuations before he'd even reached his flat.

So Rita felt scared, did she? What the hell did she think *he* felt, coming home evening after evening to this awful anomalous situa-tion, the two of them living here together neither as lovers nor as enemies, neither friends nor strangers, and never knowing what to say, how to behave? It was enough to scare anybody!

In default of anything more imaginative, he usually said, "Hello, my dear, how have you been today?" as soon as he got home, and then, while she told him, he would unload his briefcase, set out the papers on his desk, plan his work for the evening. Things were particularly busy in his department at this time of the year—in fact, "She *would* do it just now!" had been the very first thought that had flashed through his mind when he heard that she'd broken her neck. Flashed quite involuntarily, of course; people don't *choose* their first reactions to shocks like this.

"Hello, my dear, how have—" he was beginning, as usual; but this time Rita was ahead of him, interrupting, cutting across the safe little bit of routine he had so painfully managed to evolve. Very regal did she look, almost awe-inspiring, standing right in his path, straight and rigid in her plaster, like the statue of an Assyrian queen. So unexpected was the apparition, that it took him

119

a few seconds to take in what she was saying, and a few more to realise that it was something to which he couldn't just not listen.

It looked like good-bye to his evening's work, anyway. It seemed that Rita had overheard bits of his colloquy with Dorothy on the stairs, and was wild to know the rest. What had they been saying about her? What had Dorothy been telling him? And while they ate the fish pie and baked potatoes that Dorothy had left in the oven for them, Adrian found himself cornered into satisfying her curiosity. It was against all his instincts to do so, and so he answered her questions as briefly as he could, and sulkily. It wasn't that there was anything in that long-winded conversation with Dorothy that he considered worth hiding; it was just that it was all so tedious, and he was quite certain that at some point or other in the exchange Rita was going to start crying. He would find that he had said the wrong thing, insulted her in some complicated way, and the rest of the evening would have to be spent in sorting out the misunderstanding. A sort of weary boredom enveloped him, and he ate his baked potato almost without tasting it—not even bothering to split it open and put butter in. Usually (as dear old Dorothy well knew) he loved baked potatoes with butter; but this evening it seemed that he wasn't to be allowed to enjoy even that.

"Nothing much—I was simply asking her how you'd been today"—he stalled: but of course it was no use. Rita wasn't a woman to be diverted from her purpose so easily, and the ensuing interchange was like being checkmated at chess. She drove him back and back, pouncing on his every evasion, parrying every change of subject, until at last there was no way to turn, and he was cornered, compelled, against all his instincts, into asking her what it was she'd meant when she told Dorothy she was "scared"?

He didn't want to know. He didn't want to hear a thing about it. This was exactly the sort of emotional confrontation he'd been trying to avoid all these days, but having been manoeuvred into asking the question, there was no way of not hearing the answer:

"Well—wouldn't anyone be scared?" retorted Rita, with a short laugh. "I mean, when someone has had one try at murdering you, you really can't help wondering when and how the next try is coming. Can you?"

Adrian gulped. He tried to count ten before answering, but only got as far as three.

"You mean, then—you seriously mean—that all that stuff you told the newspapers was supposed to be *true?* You weren't just in a state of shock when they interviewed you—not knowing what you were saying . . . ?"

"I was in a state of shock, all right. . . ." A little smile played around the tip-tilted jaw-line atop the plaster. "Naturally I was. But I also knew what I was saying. I knew perfectly well. And it was true. That's why I said it. I *was* pushed."

She waited, lips slightly parted, for Adrian to ask the next question she had lined up for him; and something in her air of greedy expectancy made him long not to ask it. But of course he had to.

"Well, so who was it? *Who* do you think pushed you?"

The smile glinting at him over the rim of the neck-brace was horrible. From this angle, it seemed as if it, too, was supported by plaster and criss-cross metal wires. You could see that what was being led up to was something she'd been looking forward to saying for days. He watched her savouring it, the delicate tip of her tongue lightly travelling around the curved bow of her pink lips.

"*Who?* Now now, Adrian, darling, don't let's pretend! You know very well who it was. You *can't* not know!"

Adrian gritted his teeth.

"You've been talking to Derek!" he accused her. "Well, as it happens, so have I! And let me tell you, Rita—"

"To *Derek?* Oh, but darling, I wouldn't listen to *Derek!* He's half crazy with jealousy, so he can't see anything straight. Would you believe it, the poor silly man insists it was *you* who pushed me! Did you ever hear such nonsense? When he said that, I just laughed out loud, the whole ward must have wondered what the joke was! *No*, darling, of course I know it wasn't you! You haven't got it in you. And besides, you love me. . . ."

She paused a moment, watching him. Then:

"Come on, darling, guess again! You can't? You can't *really?* Well, then, let's give you a few clues, like in those party games. Who is it who hates me—who has always hated me? Who is so jealous of me that it's like a sort of illness? Who? Come on: Who? *Who?*"

Her lips smacked wetly; her eyes were alight with victory. Adrian would not speak at first, nor look at her. Then, in a sullen, harsh voice he tried one more red herring.

"Peggy?" he muttered unconvincingly, and then, raising his head, he continued clearly and decisively, "My dear Rita, you flatter yourself! If Peggy had been *that* jealous of you, she'd—"

But Rita interrupted with a sneering little laugh.

"Oh, *Peggy*!" She spoke the name witheringly, brushing it aside with contempt. "*Of course* it wasn't Peggy, the poor fish! *She* hasn't got it in her, either! Guess again, Adrian! Guess again! I'll give you just one more clue. Who is the little snow-white angel who can do no wrong? The little snow-white angel who loves her Daddy so much, with a sick, neurotic sort of love . . . ?"

Adrian took a step forward.

"Rita! Don't you dare! If you ever again so much as hint that Amelia—!"

"Oh, but darling, I won't! I'll never breathe a word of it to any living soul! I'm sorry I said as much as I did to that newspaper man; as you say, I was in a state of shock at the time—but even so, I still wouldn't reveal Amelia's name. And afterwards, for your sake, I actually took the whole thing back, pretended I hadn't known what I was saying, and that in fact I hadn't been pushed at all.

"But, Adrian, I *did* know what I was saying. I *had* been pushed. For your sake, I told a lie. And for your sake I will go on lying. I know how much your daughter means to you, and I don't want it to be through *me* that she gets sent to a special school, or a mental hospital, or whatever it is they do with child murderers. I'll shield her, Adrian, I'll keep her dreadful secret till the end of my days: but on one condition . . ."

"Shut up! If it wasn't for your bloody plaster and your goddam injuries, I'd knock you from one end of the room to the other! I'll not stand by and hear my daughter—"

"You just can't face up to it, can you, Adrian? I knew you were going to react like this. But listen. She *did* do it, and I know she did it—I was there, remember? And what's more, the silly child left incriminating evidence which luckily, it is in my power to reveal or to suppress . . ."

"Rita, you're mad!" Adrian's fury was turning to a sort of incredulous bewilderment. "You know as well as I do that Amelia *couldn't* have done it. She isn't even *at* the school at such an hour of the evening! Besides which, she has absolutely no motive of any sort—this jealousy idea is simply a load of rubbish, and you know it! I admit that right at the beginning I was afraid that she *might* be jealous, after having had me to herself for so long; but as it turned out, she wasn't. She's not the jealous type. In fact, she was beginning to be quite fond of you—hang it all, Rita, you were *trying* to make her fond of you, and you were succeeding! You were going out of your way to be nice to her—you were making a big effort, I could see you were—and I was most grateful—"

"Pity you never thought of saying so at the time!" exclaimed Rita with a sudden, heartfelt bitterness which contrasted strangely with the foregoing histrionics. Then, with a return to her former melodramatic style, she resumed:

"You say she had 'absolutely no motive'. But she had, you know. A most compelling motive."

Something in the way she spoke sent a chill through Adrian. He recognised in it the quiet confidence, the suppressed triumph of the player who really *has* got the ace of trumps in his hand.

Fear had him rattled. It brought the anger back into his voice and confused his train of thought.

"*Motive*" he blustered, "of course she hadn't a motive! What motive *could* she have had? Just tell me that. *What* motive?"

Still Rita just smiled, with that strange air of assurance. Already, her smile seemed to say, victory was in the bag. There was no hurry.

Adrian clenched his fists till the nails bit into his palms. If he had believed in prayer, he would have prayed in that moment for Rita's miraculous recovery then and there so that he could have knocked her down.

"*What* motive?" he repeated savagely; and this time Rita deigned to answer him.

"Did it never occur to you, Adrian, that your wonderful little daughter might at some time or another have done something really wicked and shameful? And that *I* might be the only person to know about it? How would *that* be for a motive? She only has to get rid of me, and she's in the clear, isn't she? And don't ask me, Adrian, *what* this shameful secret of hers was, because I'm sure you'd hate to be told. You only like hearing *nice* things about your little darling, don't you? Nice, clever, marvellous things, that prove how perfect she is! You don't want to hear the truth, and so I won't tell you. I'd hate to upset you. . . .

"But while I don't want to upset *you*, Adrian, I don't feel a bit that way about the police. Anyway, it wouldn't upset them, would it, they're used to dealing with sordid and disgusting secrets, it's part of their job. And so, if it happened that they were actually to *question* me. . . .

"No, no, Adrian, don't get hysterical! It won't come to that! I won't let it! I know how much your daughter means to you, and for your sake I will keep her murder attempt, and its sordid little motive, a complete and absolute secret, now and for ever. I'll never mention it again—but on one condition! That you let me stay with you, Adrian: that you don't throw me out. That you love me again, the way you used to do. . . ."

Tottering forwards, she propelled herself with strange, stiff tripping movements towards him. She looked like a huge mechanical doll, arms lovingly extended as though by the operation of some sort of machinery inside.

"I love you, Adrian, I love you!" she kept repeating as she came on. He raised his fists as if to ward her off, knowing all the time that he must not give her even the lightest push. His clenched knuckles whitened with the frustration.

"Shut up! *Shut up! SHUT UP!*" he yelled; and hardly had the echoes of his voice died away than there came a tap at the door, and in walked Dorothy, her face all lit up with gleeful concern.

"He *is* her boy friend, I'm certain of it!" she burst out, unable to contain her news any longer. "I'll swear he is, because do you know what?—I heard her crying! And you know how Kathy is —she always cries when she's happy, haven't you noticed? I just *had* to come up and let you know . . . !"

CHAPTER XIX

It all ended in another lecture from Dorothy about Rita's nerves.

Adrian had followed his landlady down the four flights of stairs to the basement partly to get the hell out of the crazy accusations going on above, and partly to ensure that, this time, Rita would not be able to eavesdrop on the conversation and then keep him awake half the night going on and on about it.

Dorothy settled him comfortably at her big kitchen table, at his back the pleasant warmth of the anthracite boiler, and began her little homily.

"The thing you've got to remember, Mr Summers, is that she's not over the shock yet. A *dreadful* shock it must have been for the poor young thing" (Adrian could not suppress a small smile as he noted the ease with which "That Woman!" had changed into "the poor young thing" as a result of the recent drama) "and we can't expect her to be quite entirely reasonable about it yet. It's up to the rest of us to be a bit patient with her for a while. I mean, it's no joke, is it, falling headlong down a flight of stairs, even if you *weren't* pushed! And if you keep fancying that you *were*, and brooding over it, the way she's been doing—well, it takes its toll, doesn't it? It must do."

As to this, Adrian would not commit himself. After all, it was nearly three weeks now since the accident, and quite a number of days since Rita came out of hospital, and already you could see a big improvement. She was stronger, walking more easily, moving altogether more confidently—surely it was time she pulled herself together a bit emotionally as well?

Dorothy shook her head, with an air of dark foreboding. She didn't like things to come right as simply and straightforwardly as all that; it was against Nature.

"Well, I don't know, Mr Summers, I'm sure," she said. "We mustn't look for miracles, must we, not after a dreadful accident like that? And then you must remember there was the anaesthetic and everything . . . it does funny things to a person, you know, an anaesthetic. Even just gas at the dentist's, there's some people can't take it. They go kind of funny afterwards, and start imagining things that never happened. There was this woman I once knew who swore that her dentist had been—you know—carrying on with her—going the whole way, you understand—the same time as he was taking out eight of her teeth and draining an abscess. Well, I know I'm only an old maid, and maybe my opinion's not worth much, but it did strike me—well, I mean, I did venture to doubt. . . . You know, when you start actually trying to picture it, how he could have managed . . . ? Well, anyway, to cut a long story short, I couldn't help but be a bit disbelieving—and, my goodness, did she get in a paddy! She *knew* it had happened, she said, she'd been conscious all the time and she *remembered* it! But it was all right, she said, because she loved *him*, too. . . . I forget how it all ended. I do know she was never satisfied with her plate, though. . . . Even years afterwards, she was still complaining. . . ."

"So you mean," interrupted Adrian, controlling his impatience as well as he could, "you mean that the anaesthetic they gave her might have given Rita delusions about the whole incident? Well, yes, I do agree that that's perfectly possible. It's rather along those lines that *I've* been thinking, myself—"

But Dorothy wasn't ready, just yet, to take Yes for an answer; not until the last ounce of drama had been extracted from the situation, the last shred of mystery enjoyed to the full.

"Yes, well, Mr Summers, I'm sure I hope you're right. I hope so indeed. I'd hate to think that the poor girl's fancies might have any truth in them. But if you don't mind my saying so, Mr Summers, I wouldn't just dismiss what she says as nonsense. And I wouldn't keep arguing with her about it, I really wouldn't. All this reasoning with her, and proving it can't have happened, it only puts her back up, and fixes it in her mind, like. Now, what *I* say to her when she starts on about it, I say, Yes, my dear, dreadful isn't it, all these hooligans and that, I've heard there's more muggings in the schools these days than out in the streets. And then we have a nice little chat about it all, all the rapings and the murders you read about, and it kind of takes her mind off. That way, I don't have to contradict her, and nor I don't have to say Yes, dear, I'm sure you're quite right, you *were* pushed.

"See what I mean?"

Sound psychology, no doubt. But then, Dorothy didn't know that it was Amelia who was the prime target of Rita's obsession. Had she done so, she would have undoubtedly been almost as outraged and angry as was Adrian himself; this, no doubt, was why Rita had refrained from mentioning it to her. All that Dorothy knew was that Rita was convinced that "somebody" had deliberately pushed her, and she imagined that Rita was as mystified as herself as to who this "somebody" might be.

Indeed, it was this very element of mystery that had aroused Dorothy's sympathy to the utmost.

"You can't wonder the poor young thing's just a bag of nerves can you?" she commented, setting an outsize mug of tea in front of Adrian, and providing another for herself. "I mean, think of it! To be all the time suspecting that someone is after you, trying to kill you, but never the least idea *who* it is or *why*! You can see why the poor girl hates being up in that flat by herself, can't you? She keeps thinking she hears footsteps on the stairs, she says; and of course she can't just get up and go and have a look like anyone else might, because it still takes her ever such a time to get out of her chair ... that's what's so frightening for the poor thing! She just has to sit there, waiting for there to be a knock, or for the door-handle to turn, and wondering all the time who it is, and if they've crept up deliberately, knowing that she's helpless. . . . Oh, now, I say, Mr Summers, you haven't even started your tea! It'll be getting cold!"

Adrian reached out a reluctant hand towards the jumbo-sized mug, trying to hide his distaste. He hated tea after his evening meal, coffee was the only proper beverage, and he'd been hoping, somehow, to dispose of the intimidating volume of fluid while Dorothy wasn't looking. But now, all hope of subterfuge was gone. With Dorothy's hospitable eyes beaming right at him, he lifted the mug grimly towards his lips; but before he'd steeled himself to take so much as a single sip, there came from upstairs a sudden, fearful scream.

Both of them leaped to their feet, and even as they did so there came a second scream, and a third, echoing and re-echoing down the four flights of stairs.

Now, whether it was a tribute to Adrian's coolness and presence of mind, or whether it was just one more instance of the heart-lessness with which Rita had so recently reproached him—it has to be recorded that his immediate reaction to those first terrifying seconds was to seize the opportunity to tip his tea down the sink while Dorothy's back was turned; after which he rushed immediately to see if Rita was being murdered, taking the stairs three at a time, and outdistancing the panting Dorothy almost before she was through the kitchen door. Such was his headlong speed that he almost collided with the plump youth who was supposed to be Kathy's new boy friend; but this was no time for social niceties so he charged on without apologising, up the next two flights and in through his own front door, which was ajar.

What he'd expected to find, Adrian could not have said; there simply had been no time to run through the possibilities, to conjure up pictures of blood on carpet and walls, of smashed glass and over-turned furniture. And yet, when he burst into the flat and found none of these things—the carpet still spotless from this morning's hoovering and all the furniture in place—his reaction was one of pure shock. It was like leaping from what you thought was a ten-foot wall, and finding that the ground was only two inches below you.

You feel a fool first. Then angry.

"Rita!" he called sharply—and at that moment he saw her, standing in the doorway of the bedroom, very straight in her plaster, and her eyes blinking as if in unaccustomed light. She was wearing her dark tapestry dressing-gown, her black hair hanging loose about her shoulders, so that against the darkness of the unlit bedroom she had been barely visible at first glance; her face just a greyish triangle hovering five feet above the ground.

"Rita!" he shouted again—sure, somehow, that she was tricking him, though how, or for what purpose, he could not surmise. "Rita! What is it? What's the matter?" He could see, now, that her face really *was* pale, her eyes really *were* wide with terror; and yet even now he could not get rid of the idea that he was being tricked. "What's happened? What's all the screaming in aid of?"

By this time, Dorothy had appeared on the scene, puffing and gasping from her exertions, but ready with all the warmth and reassurance in which Adrian's approach had been so singularly lacking. Within seconds she had Rita back in bed, pillows comfortably arranged behind her aching back, and then, to satisfy the still trembling girl, she set off herself on a tour of the flat, stumping from room to room, with Adrian shamefacedly in her wake, making sure that no intruder lurked under any table or inside any wardrobe—not even a miniature intruder behind the ironing-board. In the course of completing this task, she had managed also to put on the kettle; and so within a couple of minutes a hot water bottle and a cup of tea had been added to the invalid's comforts; and such was the restorative effect of all this, that Rita was by now sobbing against Dorothy's shoulder, and saying she "felt better already".

The whole thing had taken three minutes flat; and Adrian gazed at Dorothy with a sort of awe. It wasn't, actually, the sort of expertise he had any ambition to emulate—being good at this sort of thing was just looking for trouble, as anyone could see—but all the same, it *was* expertise of a sort, and as such it won from him a certain grudging admiration. Rita, with Dorothy's stout arm around her, was sobbing, but not in her usual accusing way, more like a child; and like a child, she seemed to be making an effort to obey Dorothy's instructions to "Come on, ducks, tell old Dorothy all about it."

"It" didn't, from Adrian's critical point of view, amount to very much; certainly not enough to warrant all those shrieks and screams. What had happened was this.

When Adrian had elected to follow Dorothy downstairs, Rita had felt, she claimed "very rejected"; and after crying for a little bit, and listening for Adrian to come back, she had decided to go to bed. This was a manoeuvre she could just about manage by herself now, though with difficulty; it took her, she claimed, the best part of half an hour just to settle herself comfortably under the bedclothes; and this (so she asserted) was the real cause of the trouble; she should never have been left to struggle on her own like this.

Because naturally, having expended so much time and effort on getting herself into bed, she was understandably reluctant to set to work and get herself out of it again for any but the most urgent of reasons; and so when, after a few minutes, she began to hear "a funny sort of sound in the sitting-room", she found herself extremely reluctant to go and investigate. Besides, at that stage in the affair, she naturally assumed it was Adrian, back in the flat but sulking, and not bothering to come in and see her.

Well, so all right, *she* could sulk too, if that was the way he wanted to play it; and so she did not call out, or make any move. If she lay still and silent for long *enough*, then he'd *have* to look in and see if she was all right.

But still the noises went on. Soft, rustling sounds, as of someone endlessly shuffling papers; and though of course Adrian *did* shuffle papers endlessly—it was his chief occupation in life, Rita observed tartly—all the same, about this particular shuffling there was something not quite.... Well, anyway, one way and another it began to get on Rita's nerves; and so "Adrian!" she called out. And when she'd called it again, and there was still no answer— then she really *did* begin to get frightened.

From the moment she'd called out, the sounds had ceased, completely; and she was just beginning to think she might have imagined them, when suddenly—"Thud!"—as if someone had dropped a heavy book; and then a sharp little crash.

"Adrian!" she'd shrieked again, at the top of her voice; and now the sounds were unmistakable—a swift padding of stockinged feet across the sitting-room floor ... the creaking of a door ... a stir of air ... and it was at this point that Rita had really begun to scream. And scream, and scream, and scream. She must somehow have got herself out of bed at the same time, because the next thing she knew she was standing at the door of the bedroom watching Adrian burst in through the front door....

There were a dozen questions Adrian would have liked to ask; indeed he began asking them, but only to find that once again he was being a heartless monster. He had thought that he was being helpful in seeking to resolve the mystery, but evidently this was not the case.

"Can't you *see* how upset she is, the poor dear?" Dorothy reproached him, tightening her arm protectively round the invalid; and Rita began sobbing all over again, and pointing out that if only Adrian wasn't so selfish, leaving her all on her own day in and day out, then none of this would ever have happened.

It is a well-known philosophical principle that there is no way of disproving an "if" statement; but there is unquestionably a wrong time for trying to do so; and Adrian, as usual, had chosen it. With Rita in tears, and Dorothy against him too, there was nothing to be done but to drop the subject; and in any case another, quite different argument had by now blown up, with Rita urging, tearfully, that Dorothy should stay the night in the flat.

"You could sleep on the couch in the sitting-room," she pleaded. "It's quite comfortable. I wouldn't feel frightened at all if *you* were here!"

One in the eye for Adrian! Or so it sounded. Dorothy hesitated, glancing at him sidelong, to see how he was taking it.

Very badly, to judge by appearances. But Dorothy was wrong in supposing that it was the blow to his male pride that had brought the dark look to his face. What he was actually thinking was that with Dorothy on the sitting-room couch, he himself would be forced back into the double bed, which he hadn't occupied since Rita's return from hospital. The prospect of spending the night with the neck-brace, the tears, and the recriminations was more than he could stand.

He was polite, but firm. He explained to Dorothy that Rita needed the whole of the double bed to herself at the moment— that she needed to be able to shift her weight, to turn herself at this angle and at that: and he explained to Rita that they had already trespassed more than enough on Dorothy's kindness, without asking this favour of her as well. And as to Rita's fears—well, *he* was going to be here, wasn't he? Did they really think he would prove incapable of dealing with an intruder into his own flat, should the need arise?

"Everything will be perfectly all right. There's nothing whatever to worry about," he promised them both, and with this assurance, Dorothy heaved herself from her chair and took herself off downstairs.

But less than two hours later—just before one in the morning —Rita was screaming again. Screaming, and screaming, and screaming; and when Adrian, dazed with sleep, rushed to her bedside, she still did not stop.

"She's here! I saw her! She's come to kill me!" she shrieked, and nothing Adrian could do would quiet her, until, in the end, as a very last resort, he put his hand over her mouth and held it there.

CHAPTER XX

"SCREAMING? NO, I didn't hear any screaming," said Kathy vaguely; and Adrian, trying to sneak off to work as if nothing had happened, could have hugged her. If Kathy, in the room just below them, hadn't heard the screams, then the screams themselves began to seem just a little bit less real, a little bit less demanding of attention from a busy man.

And it wasn't as if Rita had been able to give any plausible explanation for her terror—if terror it was, and not just another attention-getting ploy, which was what he was beginning to suspect. When she had finally calmed down enough for him to risk taking his hand off her mouth and let her speak, the things she had to say were such a jumble of *non sequiturs* and blatant melodrama, that he could only conclude that either she had been dreaming, or that she was deliberately making a fool of him.

"I heard her! I heard her tiptoeing about again!" were Rita's first intelligible words. "She came and leaned right over me, peering into my face, but I kept my eyes tight shut, I pretended to be asleep ... and so presently she crept away again. Then, a minute later, I heard her at my handbag, I heard the clasp go, and then I heard her scratching and rustling among my things. I know what she was looking for—but Adrian, it's all lies! I promise you it's all lies ...! She's just trying to make you hate me ...!"

"Who is? What lies? What the hell are you talking about?" But Rita gabbled on, ignoring him.

"And then she was in the kitchen! I heard her! She was trying to be ever so quiet, but *I* heard her! Opening cupboards ... pulling out drawers! And then, somehow, I knew that she'd opened the knife drawer ... that she was getting out the carving knife...! And that was when I screamed, Adrian! I couldn't help it! I was so frightened!"

Until the bit about the carving knife, Adrian had been following the narrative with some degree of concern, conceiving it possible that there *might* have been an intruder going through the place; what with Dorothy's well-known habit of leaving the back door unlocked at all hours, such an occurrence was far from impossible. But the knife business made it clear that the whole thing had been merely a nightmare; and Adrian told her so, though not unkindly. She was still an invalid, and therefore entitled to deprive other people of their much-needed sleep whenever she liked, and for the silliest reasons.

To pacify her, he made a tour of the flat, ending up with a particularly careful inspection of the kitchen.

It looked all right. The drawers and cupboards were all shut, the surfaces clear. In fact, it looked a good deal tidier than it normally did, Dorothy being a more meticulous housewife than Rita.

He duly reported all this to the invalid with the intention of reassuring her; but of course it did nothing of the kind; once again, he had put his foot in it.

So he was criticising her housekeeping now, was he? He preferred that doddering old woman downstairs, did he? What sort of a lover is it who walks into his mistress's bedroom in the middle of the night and starts telling her off about the state of the kitchen when she is lying there ill and nearly paralysed? When *other* women are ill and nearly paralysed, their lovers will....

Other women! ... Other women! How it brought back those rows with Peggy! Did *nothing* ever change, no matter what you did with your life or who you shared it with?

Cold and exhausted, he sat on the end of the bed, hunched in his dressing-gown as though sheltering from a storm, and let the words drum against his skull. By dawn, he was so weary that he couldn't make out whether she was objecting to being murdered in her bed or to the fact that he never brought her roses now "like you used to do".

Used he to? He supposed so. But Rita had been different then ... exciting, inaccessible, and not constantly in tears. Or if she had, then the tears had been Derek's fault, not his, and it had been lovely. In those days it had been Derek who didn't bring her roses, didn't understand her, wouldn't listen to her, always had his nose in his books, making notes about rare and coveted plants far into the night, until (as Rita had sourly remarked) you'd have thought he couldn't tell the difference between a woman and a spider-orchid!

How they had laughed at that! Derek and his spider-orchids had become one of those sweet jokes between them. One of them only had to mention the word, and they'd be in fits of laughter for half the evening, pulling Derek to pieces, delighting in every detail of his hilarious shortcomings.

What fun it had been! No wonder he had brought her roses! If he had.

"I'll bring you some tomorrow," he promised, yawning, trying to buy a couple of hours sleep; but of course it didn't work. Soon she was accusing him of not caring whether she was murdered or not, which just at the moment he didn't, except that it would all be so exhausting, police and doctors and mortuaries and things.

Naturally, after such a night as this, the sight of Kathy, fresh-faced, no responsibility of his, some other chap's baby balanced on her hip, and with no word of blame on her rosy lips about last night's uproar, appeared to him like something straight out of heaven. He hoped, with a rush of irrelevant gratitude, that everything was going marvellously for her with this new boy friend of hers. Certainly, she looked blooming enough, and it was lovely to see a girl not crying.

"Oh, well, I'm glad it didn't disturb you," he said gratefully. "I was afraid we must have woken you up." (Actually, he hadn't given Kathy a thought at the time, he had been much too preoccupied, but the goodwill he was feeling towards her now made his words near enough to the truth.) "It was—well, you know. One of those things."

Yes, Kathy knew all right. None better. Her nineteen years had so far encompassed rather more than their share of "those things", and she nodded with heartfelt sympathy.

"No, I didn't hear a thing," she reassured him. "But then, you know, screaming never *does* bother me, unless it's *him*"—she gestured, with a small hoisting-up of his fat bottom, to the baby propped on her hip. "It's a funny thing, that. There could be an earthquake, and the whole street screaming, and I'd most likely sleep through it: but the tiniest whimper from *him*, and I'm awake in a flash! We mothers are like that, you know. It's a sort of instinct."

There was a note of unaccustomed pride in her voice, as though the idea that there was such a thing as a maternal instinct, and that she, Kathy, was partaking of it, was a new one to her, and delightful.

Adrian nodded agreement, but did not pursue the topic. This was no moment for involving himself in a discussion of maternal drives and the part they must have played in human evolution. Indeed, there wasn't much to discuss; you only had to look at that damp, demanding, grizzling creature with dribbles of egg-yolk down its chin to know that without some such overwhelming and unreasoning instinct, the human species could never possibly have survived.

He smiled at Kathy, and proceeded on his way downstairs. All he wanted, right now, was to get safely out of the house before anything else happened. Rita was asleep at the moment, but there was no knowing how long she would remain so. It wasn't as if he was leaving her unattended; Dorothy was here. Dorothy liked happenings, so let them happen away while *she* was in charge, not while he was.

Cautiously as a burglar, he slipped out through the front door, and closed it again softly behind him. Down the front steps on soundless feet: and then—freedom! Away into the damp anonymous morning! Away into the law-abiding rush-hour crowds, who moved so meekly, so predictably, along their given ways, who never screamed in the night, or got themselves pushed down flights of stairs, or landed themselves, unasked, on reluctant lovers!

Well, probably they didn't, you couldn't really tell, but let's assume they didn't! Not one single one of them! Adrian braked, and gestured with a flourish of exaggerated courtesy to the pedestrian waiting at the zebra crossing, ushering the old chap across the road as if he was royalty, and all because he never screamed in the night, or burst into tears, or fell down flights of stairs. Or, if he did, he didn't drag *Adrian* into it, the excellent old soul!

"Don't often meet *that* sort of courtesy on the roads, these days," mused the old man, grinning at Adrian and saluting with his stick as he hobbled across; and even a couple of hours later, dozing in the Public Library over the Sports Page of the Daily Mail, he was still experiencing faint echoes of what it feels like to be a V.I.P.

Before he started on his day's work, there were two calls that Adrian had to make on his office phone. He'd saved them till now because he didn't want either Rita or Dorothy breathing down his neck while he made them. Nor, come to that, did he want his secretary, so he sent her into the outer office; then he sat at his desk for a moment, his head in his hands, reminding himself of the points to be covered.

First, there was the child Daphne, who always travelled home from school with Amelia, and was Amelia's great friend. From her, he wanted a statement that on that fatal afternoon Amelia had left school at her usual time and had gone straight home by her usual route. From his ex-wife Peggy, he wanted confirmation that Amelia had arrived home on that day not later than usual. These two separate bits of information would between them eliminate all possibility that Amelia could have been in the school building at all at the time of the accident. Not that Adrian himself felt the faintest shadow of fear lest his daughter had been implicated in the thing; he just knew she hadn't. But he wanted to have some concrete evidence with which he could confront Rita and thus silence her ridiculous accusations once and for all. He had no intention of enduring yet another night of trying to counter this ridiculous, trumped-up nonsense about his daughter—a schoolgirl of thirteen—creeping around her father's flat with intent to murder! The sheer silliness of the charge made him wonder, for a moment, if it was worth refuting; but yes, of course it was. Either Rita herself actually believed it—as the result perhaps, of some shock-induced hallucination—or else she had some malicious reason for pretending that she did. Either way, the sooner she was confronted with concrete proof to the contrary, the better. He would write down, in a business-like way, exactly what Daphne said, and exactly what Peggy said too. If Rita chose still not to believe these statements, then she could just ring both witnesses herself—he would stand over her while she did it—and with her own ears hear them repeat their evidence.

Daphne's number, he knew, was somewhere at the back of his diary, because he had several times had to ring up and make arrangements about fetching Amelia from there; but it took him a minute or two to find it, because he had forgotten the child's surname. He had to go right through as far as the R's before coming to it.

Rolandson. Yes, that was it. He remembered now.

He dialled the number, and by good luck it was Daphne herself who answered; he hadn't looked forward to having to make some laborious explanation to a baffled parent before he could get through to the daughter.

But this, as it happened, was the last bit of luck he was to have that morning.

No, Daphne told him, in a small, surprised voice, no, actually she *hadn't* travelled home with Amelia on that particular day. Yes, that's right, she usually did, but Amelia hadn't come to school at all that day; she'd been absent, and so Daphne couldn't really tell him anything. She was awfully sorry, but she just didn't know a thing, because term had ended only a few days later, and Amelia still hadn't been back. . . .

Stalemate. Oh, well, never mind, there was still Peggy, and her evidence would now be even more conclusive. If Amelia had been ill that day, then Peggy would almost certainly have stayed at home from work to look after her, and would be able to vouch for her having been at home for every moment of the time. Her evidence would now by itself be entirely sufficient.

He had already dialled Peggy's work number and heard the first of the ringing tones, before he suddenly remembered: and slammed the receiver down.

Hell! Peggy wouldn't be there! She was on holiday, she had taken Amelia down to Seaford for a fortnight.

Damn, damn, damn! Now he would have to ring her at Seaford—hunt up the code-number of the place, and all the rest of the bother. And indeed he had already looked up the code-number, and had his forefinger poised to start dialling, before he realised he was up against yet another obstacle.

Where was it the two of them were staying? He racked his brains; he leafed through the pages of his diary. Had Peggy given him an address? Had he asked her for one? He simply couldn't remember. He couldn't even remember if it was a hotel they'd been going to, or ordinary seaside lodgings.

He cursed himself for not having taken more trouble about it all. Fancy a father letting his only child go away on holiday without even bothering to find out her address! The truth was that, even since the divorce, he always left this sort of thing to Peggy. Whatever her failings as a wife (and Adrian had wondered at times whether it wasn't people's virtues rather than their failings that make them impossible to live with) Peggy had always been a careful and loving mother; he had never at any time experienced one moment's anxiety about Amelia when she was in her mother's care. This, inevitably, had enabled him to be slack and inattentive about little things like dates and addresses and phone numbers. Peggy always told him, without being asked, anything like this that he ought to know.

Only this time, she hadn't.

And then again, when she went on holiday Amelia always wrote to him on the very first day, a long gabbling scrawl of impressionistic description and highly individualistic comment on the novel environment; most amusing and interesting letters, which he preserved in a special folder.

Only this time, she hadn't either.

They must have been gone for at least a week, and he hadn't heard a thing, or even wondered about them. And now here was the Easter weekend coming up, during which there *couldn't* be any letters!

Damn, damn, damn!

CHAPTER XXI

BUT AT LEAST, when he got home that evening, there had been no more footsteps—or, if there had, they were keeping them from him, thank goodness.

Maybe it was cowardly of him, but he hadn't gone straight up to the flat when he got in, but had slipped off down to the basement to have a word with Dorothy first. Not that Dorothy's account of the day's doings could be a hundred percent relied on—far from it. But then, that was the whole point of coming to her first. Whatever she told him, he'd know that at least it wasn't as bad as *that*, and so would be able to go up and face the reality in the comforting knowledge that it could have been worse.

That Dorothy's report might prove to be wholly favourable, had simply never crossed his mind; and for a moment it quite threw him.

Yes, Rita seemed a lot better today, Dorothy told him, glancing up from her copy of *Vogue* in an uncharacteristically off-hand manner. Yes, she'd managed to dress herself, and this afternoon had even gone out for a little walk. Yes, outside. In the street.

"That's good," commented Adrian warily, and waited for Dorothy to tell him what had gone wrong. That the poor young thing had come back looking as white as a sheet? That Dorothy had had to help her up the steps and give her a drop of brandy to calm her nerves? That, in Dorothy's opinion, the poor silly girl was rushing things too much, was overdoing it—this opinion, of course, being backed by appropriate anecdotes of the multifarious disasters which had befallen acquaintances of Dorothy's who, over the years, had "overdone it" in various assorted ways after various assorted illnesses and mishaps?

You should watch her, Mr Summers, see that she takes things a bit more slowly—he waited for Dorothy to admonish him thus darkly—and when she didn't, he had a sense of disorientation.

"You mean she managed to come down all those stairs by herself?" he asked—almost prompting Dorothy to restore normality by some doomful pronouncement on the probable outcome of the rash escapade. But all she said was, "Yes, she must have done, mustn't she? Soon be quite herself again, won't she, at this rate?"

For a minute or two more, Adrian hung about in the doorway, unable to believe that this was really the end of the day's news. It was like opening your morning paper and reading the headlines:

"MILLIONS CROSS THE ROAD IN SAFETY"
"DOCTOR SAYS THOUSANDS NOT SUFFERING FROM STRESS"

Was Dorothy ill, he wondered? Or annoyed about something? And why wasn't she urging him to sit down, to stay and chat for a minute, and to drink one of those awful mugs of tea? Admittedly, he nearly always refused, or else cursed himself for the waste of time if he accepted; but simply not to be *asked* was quite another matter. He stood for a few moments more, quite ridiculously hurt and put out; and then, because there seemed nothing else to do, he turned and made his way upstairs.

Rita must have been tired out by her unaccustomed exertions, because when Adrian came into the flat, everything was silent, and it seemed that she was asleep. Either that, or she was sulking—anyway, the bedroom door was shut, and there was no sound from behind it. For a few moments, Adrian stood, in deep thought: then, bracing himself, he decided to leave well alone, and went straight to his desk. He'd been longing for a chance to sort out the pile of stuff that had accumulated there during these last traumatic days, and this really seemed to be the moment he'd been waiting for. Of course, if Rita *was* only sulking, and was lying there listening to his every movement, then of course there'd be hell to pay; but a man has to take *some* risks, some of the time, if he is to salvage any life of his own at all. Besides, he could always say he'd *thought* she was asleep, and was afraid of disturbing her. And in any case, Dorothy would be up soon, organising some sort of a meal for them, and that would provide a diversion. He'd press Dorothy to stay and eat with them; you can't really quarrel in a threesome—or, if you do, it is not nearly so painful. *Someone*, willy-nilly, becomes pig-in-the-middle, deflecting the sharpest of the blows from either direction.

But Dorothy didn't come. The clock ticked; Adrian's waste-paper basket gradually filled up with all those so-recently precious documents which had somehow become rubbish while no one was noticing; and still no sound came from the bedroom.

He was growing hungry. Of course, there was no actual reason why Dorothy *should* cook their meal for them, evening after evening, but she'd been doing it for so many days now that Adrian found himself feeling really quite aggrieved at this sudden lapse.

He thought of going into the kitchen and opening a tin of roast chicken, or something, but immediately realised that if he did this he would be more or less compelled to offer some to Rita. He would have to go into the bedroom, find out if she was hungry, sick, cross, better, worse, crying, sulking, remorseful, affectionate. . . . The intensity with which he didn't want to know any of these things was like an illness; so he dismissed the idea of the tinned chicken, and went on with his sorting.

By eight o'clock, the waste-paper basket was full to overflowing, and Adrian went downstairs to empty it. He was surprised, as he went through the kitchen en route for the dustbins, that Dorothy, usually so eager for a chat with anyone at any time, hardly looked up; and when he reached the back door, he got another shock.

The back door was locked. *Locked!*

It was easy enough to unfasten; that wasn't the problem. He lurched back into the kitchen like a man in shock.

"*Dorothy!*" he exclaimed, "You've locked the back door! Whatever have you done that for?"

Dorothy looked at him over the top of her gold-rimmed spectacles. There was a sort of smug, wary slyness about her. She pointed out, entirely reasonably, that it was Adrian himself who'd been urging her for years—ever since he came here, in fact—to do just this. Especially since the business of the squatters, he'd been going on at her about how she ought to lock the back door.

And now she'd locked it. So what about it?

What indeed? Everything she said was absolutely true, and incontrovertible. How could one set against such unexceptionable logic the awful sense of shock, of personal affront, which had assailed Adrian when he'd shoved at the door in the old, familiar relaxed way, and it hadn't swung open for him?

It was an absurd feeling! It was beyond all sense and reason! As Dorothy had just reminded him, it was he himself who had been telling her for years what a fool she was to leave the door unlocked. He'd even, after the episode of the squatters, had a key cut for her himself, and had muttered imprecations on her when he found that she'd just shoved the key to the back of the knife drawer, and never used it at all.

Blithering old fool, he'd thought! Putting the whole household at risk with her damn carelessness!

And so whence, now, came this overwhelming feeling that with the locking of the back door, some awful disintegration was beginning? That some vital centre of the house had suddenly fallen apart, leaving them all defenceless?

It was this word "defenceless" coming into his mind that brought Adrian to his senses. For obviously, it is leaving doors *unlocked* that renders people defenceless, not the other way round. He pulled himself together, apologised to Dorothy, handsomely admitting the rightness of her arguments; and then, retracing his steps to the back door, he turned the key, still stiff and shiny with newness, and let himself out into the black, windy night. On his return, with the empty basket, he carefully re-locked the door and set off on his return journey—the first lap of which took him, of course, through the kitchen once again.

Usually, he traversed this stretch of the terrain as rapidly as possible. It was a sort of race, actually, with Dorothy trying to capture his interest in what she was saying faster than he could get across the room and out through the further door. Sometimes, she succeeded, and then he would sigh, lean up against the door frame, and wait while she regaled him with the latest state of play between Kathy and Brian; or maybe about the gas being cut off at Number Twenty-two up the road just when the old lady was sick with pneumonia, and when they'd come to turn it on again and say they were sorry the boy had said What old lady?—because of course being Australian he'd been out with his pals every single evening and didn't know who was in the house and who wasn't, you know what these Aussies are. . . .

Always, it would sound as if *this* was the climax of the story . . . or this . . . or this . . . but it never was. Always, there was more of the tale still to come. It was like mountain-climbing, with those further, higher peaks for ever appearing ahead just when you think you have reached the top. . . .

How boring it all was, he'd tell himself; how he longed for her to get to the end of the thing and release him!

But tonight, the tables seemed to be well and thoroughly turned. He found himself actually *missing* her chatter; actually trying, inexpertly, to set her going again, as if she was a run-down machine.

For it was unheard of for Dorothy to be like this! It was against nature! Something obstinate and pertinacious arose in Adrian, and he determined, precious though his time was, to stay down here and *force* things back into their normal course; to *make* Dorothy be herself again.

How were the Brewers, he asked her, sitting himself down uninvited at the kitchen table? Had they managed to patch things up after leaving here? And what about the Harveys?—and Mrs Worsley??—and That Miss Evans?—mentioning at random the names of various ex-lodgers whose most intimate and private concerns had at various times over the past years hummed like gnats on summer evenings through this superbly well-documented kitchen.

No. Nothing much. Not lately. I haven't seen her.

But Adrian was not to be put off by these discouraging and un-Dorothy-like replies. He tried again.

How about the Squatters? Had she seen anything more of them? One of them, if he remembered rightly, had come back a few days after the great exodus to ask Dorothy if she'd seen anything of his leather cycling gloves, and had written out for her, with a stubby, almost illegible bit of pencil, an address to which they could be sent.

At the mention of the Squatters, a faint quiver of response could be discerned in Dorothy's slumped pose, and she exerted herself to remark that this was the *third* lot of builders that had come to look at the Squatters' Flat, and these building firms, they're all the same these days, you can't count on them for anything.

"They come and look at the place," she complained, "and they say they'll send in an estimate, and then that's the last you hear of them! It's beginning to get me down, Mr Summers, it really is! Sometimes I wonder why I'm running this place at all! All the work . . . and the worry . . . I sometimes wonder what I'm doing it all *for*."

This un-Dorothy-like sentiment could not be allowed to pass for one moment: Adrian fought for the return of her Dorothy-ness as if for his life.

Of course there was a point in what she was doing, he assured her. Apart from anything else, didn't she realise how important she was to them all?—how attached they all were to her? Why, he couldn't imagine how any of them could manage without her at all. Look at all she'd been doing for *him* this last couple of weeks, looking after Rita so splendidly; he just didn't know how he could have coped without her. And not just these last two weeks, either, she'd been marvellous all these four years, really she had; and look how fond Amelia was of her.

He could see, by the end of his speech, that she was beginning to feel just a bit better—as who wouldn't be under such a barrage of praise and appreciation?—and so he pressed on.

"And Kathy, too," he reminded her. "The way you look after that baby for her, and listen to all her troubles! The number of times I've found her down here, crying, and you cheering her up, and lending her packets of things, and taking messages for her boy friends...!"

"Well, I do my best, I suppose," said Dorothy, plainly a little bit mollified, but still glum. "And that's another thing, Mr Summers! That Kathy! She hasn't been down here for days! I don't know what's going on up there at all, I really don't! You know that new boy friend of hers I've been seeing around—the one I told you about? You saw him yourself one time, remember, and you agreed with me that he seemed more the steady type? Well, it looks like he's not her boy friend at all—not any more, anyhow! Isn't it a shame? I saw him with my own eyes, I happened to be looking up through the banisters, and I saw him going out of the door with quite a different girl! Holding hands, they were, and slipping out as if they didn't want anyone to know! A good-looker she was, I will say that, long blonde hair down to her waist—well nearly blonde—and lovely blue eyes! Determined-looking, too. *She'll* get him, I said to myself; our Kathy'll never stand a chance against *that* one! She's not a fighter, Kathy's not, that's always been her trouble... she lets them walk all over her..."

In vain did Adrian point out that Kathy's relationship with this nameless boy might well have been a figment of Dorothy's imagination right from the start. After all, Dorothy had never actually *seen* them together, had she? Well, then. Probably he and this girl were just a couple of friends of hers and Brian's....

At this, Dorothy's face darkened.

"Don't talk to me about That Brian!" she commanded. "If it wasn't for *him*, Kathy'd have found herself a nice, steady fellow long ago! If only he'd go away and *stop* away, not all this coming and going and messing her about! He knows she's crazy about him, she'll never turn him away no matter how he treats her, he knows that: though let me tell you, if *I* was a young girl like her, in her position, I mean...."

With a leap of joy in his heart which quite startled him by its intensity, Adrian realised suddenly that the old Dorothy was back! Somehow, somewhere, during the course of this diatribe, she had quietly returned! Already, she was on her feet, putting the kettle on, while at the same time describing in colourful detail exactly what would by now have befallen That Brian if she, Dorothy, had been the lady in the case.

And this time, Adrian drank his daunting mug of tea as if it was nectar, drank it right up, as a sort of small thank-offering to the gods for restoring Dorothy-ness to the world again.

It was shortly after this that he noticed that it was ten o'clock already. Had they really been talking that long?—Rita would be furious! There was really no chance at all that she would still be asleep after all this time. Taking his leave of Dorothy—a good deal more warmly than usual because of his gratitude to her for being herself after her brief but alarming abdication from the rôle —he sped off upstairs. He noticed, as he went, how very quiet the house seemed to be tonight. The ground-floor flat, naturally, was quiet, for there was as yet no one in it; but so too, when he reached that landing, was Kathy's. No crooning from the radio— no crying baby—no voices raised in argument or laughter. His own flat, too, when he walked into it, was absolutely silent; and this time he really *was* puzzled. Surely Rita couldn't *still* be asleep— or, alternatively, still sullenly lying there, waiting for him to make the first move? He strode swiftly to the bedroom and flung open the door.

It was empty. The bed, though rumpled and unmade, had obviously been empty for some time. It was quite cold. And on one of the pillows lay what he was by now naturally looking for—a note.

I can't stand another night of this, [he read] the constant terror, the constant listening for footsteps—and so I am going away. I am in *danger* here. I know you don't believe it, Adrian, because you don't *want* to believe it, but your daughter intends to kill me. Each night she grows more daring—I dare not stay here any longer.

I know, Adrian, what you are thinking. You are thinking that I'm deluded, that Amelia *can't* be creeping about the flat at night because she's away at Seaford with her mother.

But is she? How do you know? Have you heard from her? Or from her mother? How do you know that they ever went away at all?

I sometimes wonder, Adrian, whether you know *anything* about *anybody*! That's the trouble with being as selfish as you are—you never think about other people, and so of course you never learn anything about them. So you end up not knowing anything at all, about any of us.

Rita.

CHAPTER XXII

SHEER, INCREDULOUS RELIEF at first blotted out all other considerations.

She was gone! She was actually *gone*! Such luck, so soon, had been beyond his wildest dreams. Crumpling the note into a tight ball, he tossed it into the air for the sheer joy of it, and batted it with the flat of his hand into the newly-emptied waste-paper basket.

It landed dead centre. Perfect! He laughed aloud, and flung himself full-length on the spacious, unmade bed, his own again at last!

Freedom! Freedom! At last, after all these weeks, the bed was his, the flat was his. His very life was his own again, to live exactly as he chose. It was like being let out of prison, it was like recovering from a long illness—and with the Easter weekend just coming up too, so that on top of all this freedom, he would be having a holiday as well.

Tomorrow was Good Friday. It would be succeeded by Saturday, Sunday and Monday, all official holidays. For four whole days he would not have to drive to work, to keep his temper, to suffer fools, to agree with nonsense, or to consider anyone's convenience at all except his own! Just as some men need to go on the bottle every so often in order to get a break from ordinary life and ordinary civilised behaviour, so did Adrian need an occasional orgy of pure, uncomplicated solitude. With four whole days ahead of him, he could go on a real bender, going to bed when he liked, getting up when he liked, reading all night with the light on and no one to complain about it. Reading all day, too, if he chose, without anyone saying, "But I thought you said that after lunch we were going to . . .?" He could do what he liked without anyone arguing; he could think what he liked without anyone saying "You mean you don't love me?"

It was intoxicating! It was like winning the Pools! He went to bed in a state of mindless euphoria, comparable to that of a seven-year-old on the night before his birthday—the one, magic night of the year when all the toys in the world are within his grasp, from an electric train set to a working model of a moon-rocket.

But of course—as with winning the Pools—this first, carefree euphoria cannot last. For a few hours, perhaps—at most a day—the joy is pure and unsullied; then, relentlessly, the problems set in.

By morning (he hadn't, after all, been reading all night, but sleeping like a log for eight and a half hours)—by morning, the ecstasy was gone, and the problems, small and large, were buzzing round his newly-awakened head like a swarm of mosquitoes.

What should he *tell* everybody—that was the first question. Last night, in the first flush of relief and joy, he had planned to tell no one at all, to hug the thing to himself as a precious secret, and to revel in his miraculous and unpremeditated solitude as if it was a secret vice.

But now, in the harsh light of 8.15 am, he realised how totally impractical was this project. Rita would probably have been on the phone to half their friends and acquaintances already, in tears, and giving her side of the story: which was rather unfair, when you came to think of it, because what *his* side of the story was he had no idea, and therefore couldn't retaliate in kind.

Who should he tell, then? And how? Certainly, he would have to tell Dorothy, and tell her quickly, otherwise she would be coming up as usual this morning to tidy round and help Rita to get dressed. And as soon as he had dealt with this—and had listened to her flood of reproaches, lamentations and forebodings concerning the whole matter—then he would straightaway have to tackle the problem of Rita's things. He wasn't going to keep them here another day if he could help it.

He shut his eyes, and buried his face in the pillow so as not to have to see them any more; but he still had to think about them in order to make his plans. He could see them in his mind's eye all too clearly; her clothes, her make-up, her bottles and jars of this and that. Her clothes-brush, her scent spray—and, of course, far worse than these relatively portable objects were the bits and pieces of furniture and equipment that had been seeping insidiously, week by week, into the flat. The oval mirror, of course, had been broken, so that was one problem solved; but the cut-glass fruit bowl hadn't, nor all those imitation Wedgwood plates and dishes which now cluttered up the handsome oak sideboard. And then there was her bedside table, varnished a hideous yellowy colour, and the candlesticks, and the china model of Bambi. There were her hair-curlers too, and the squalid cretonne box containing powder, lipstick and dirty hairnets. There was her steam-iron, and her clogged-up carpet sweeper, and her hanging wardrobe of transparent plastic—oh, a million things! Until they were gone, he couldn't really feel free of her. He was aware, suddenly, of the hidden power of mere objects. It was as if they'd grown a faint, sticky web around them during the night in which they planned to entangle him, and hold him a helpless captive, until it should please her to return. . . .

The very air seemed full of threats. Lifting his head from the pillow, he forced himself to open his eyes. He looked from the beside table to the sunray lamp; from the hair-drier to the imitation crocodile boots; and then scrambled apprehensively out of bed as if some doomful gong had sounded somewhere.

Fortunately for Adrian, telling Dorothy what had happened and arranging for the packing up of Rita's belongings turned out to be one and the same task, more or less.

"But what about her *things*, Mr Summers?" had been Dorothy's first and entirely spontaneous reaction to the dramatic news of Rita's disappearance; and it was immediately followed by an offer to come up "right away" and help him get them packed.

Adrian couldn't have thought up a more convenient reaction on his landlady's part if he'd tried for a year; but all the same, he was shocked.

Didn't she *care*? *He* didn't care, naturally; in fact quite the contrary, but that was different. *Someone* ought to care, and in this case Dorothy was the obvious person, she having befriended Rita so assiduously of late. She *must* care, it was her duty to care, if only as an antidote to his own ruthless unconcern. There should be a proper balance in these things, with some people reliably feeling the right feelings, in order to make a solid basis from which other people could safely feel the wrong ones.

It did cross his mind, as Dorothy laboured her way upstairs in front of him, that Dorothy and Rita might have plotted the whole thing between them, which of course would explain Dorothy's unconcern as well as her astounding lack of curiosity. He knew that Dorothy could be very cunning sometimes, and very devious. He knew also that, when it suited her, she could lie fluently and without the smallest qualms of conscience, and so it wouldn't be the least use asking her anything.

At one time, it had struck him as odd, not to say paradoxical, that someone as untrustworthy as Dorothy should have so many people queueing up to confide in her their darkest secrets; and it had taken him some months to realise that actually there was no incongruity in this at all. A person who can tell lies easily and without guilt is actually a far more trustworthy confidante than an honest person, who is bound by the truth. Confronted by a straight yes-or-no question from some third party, the honourable truth-teller will have no option but to answer truthfully—i.e. to give away your confidences. Whereas an accomplished liar, once she is on your side, can be relied on to keep your secret through thick and thin; she will tell, competently and without batting an eyelid, all the lies that are necessary to keep you out of trouble. To be a liar is not at all the same thing as to be untrustworthy; quite the contrary.

What Dorothy's motive could have been in involving herself in this conspiracy to get Rita out of the house without his knowledge (if indeed she had done so) he could not guess, and he had no intention of trying. Motives are usually mixed, and only partially conscious; and the unravelling of them, in Adrian's experience, was liable to be not only fruitless, but tedious in the extreme.

Anyway, Dorothy was a marvellous help with the packing. All those tasks that to him seemed so distasteful—fingering through the garments in the wardrobe, collecting shoes and boots together from here, there and everywhere—under the bed, behind bits of furniture—all this Dorothy undertook with gusto, contributing a running commentary the while on where each item might have been bought, and when, and what had been its probable price. All that Adrian had to do, really, was to help with lifting the heavier things, and to carry rubbish down those long flights of stairs to the dustbins. The back door, he noted with wry amusement, was no longer locked; in fact, it was swinging wide open, filling the house with swirling draughts from the wild April day outside.

By evening, the cases and boxes were all packed, the pieces of furniture done up with brown paper and string. All that remained now was to ring up a removal firm first thing in the morning, and have them sent off to—

Well, where? And now at last Adrian was up against the crunch, which he had been trying to avoid thinking about all day.

He did not know where she had gone. Presumably she was either at her mother's or at Derek's—but which? He dared not ring either address for fear that she *was* there, and would answer the phone, and the thought of hearing her voice, of having to make actual contact with her after all that had happened, just simply terrified him.

He could ring Derek of course, at work, but that could not happen until Tuesday. No one would be working now until after the weekend—three more whole days to get through with all those boxes and things lined up waiting, an ever-present threat, a reminder that she *could*—oh, yes, she *could*—change her mind and come back. She could do it tonight. Or tomorrow. Any time. Until her belongings—every last tube of face-cream and jar of eye-liner— were out of the house, there was no security. He was like a man under suspended sentence.

He spent a restless, uneasy weekend, neither enjoying the holiday nor getting down to any solid work. Every time he heard a step on the stair . . . a car drawing up outside the house . . . he would find himself in a sweat of apprehension. His anxiety began to invade even his dreams. Twice—three times—on the Saturday night he woke, fancying that some disturbance in the flat had woken him. Once, he even thought he heard the sound of one of those heavy suitcases being dragged across the floor, and he'd leapt out of bed in absolute horror, his half-awakened mind full of visions of Rita in there in the sitting-room, quietly and methodically unpacking everything in the dark, releasing her belongings once more into his flat, like plague bacilli from some Science Fiction laboratory. . . .

But of course, there was nothing. The boxes and cases, the corded-up furniture, were still piled as he and Dorothy had left them, looming like monsters startled into immobility by the sudden light. Coming out on to the landing, and in the very moment of switching on the light, he'd fancied he'd caught a glimpse of flying hair disappearing round the banisters, vanishing into the darkness of the floor below; but when he thought back to this moment afterwards, he could not be sure it had not been the tail-end of one of his dreams. Anyway, it hadn't been black hair, like Rita's, it had been lightish, almost fair, if it had existed at all.

He searched the flat in every corner, and even explored the rest of the house, right down to the kitchen, but without result. He took the opportunity of locking the back door while he was about it— evidently, Dorothy was right back on form now, he reflected wryly —and made his way back to bed.

But it was a long while before he could sleep. The sky was already growing light before the fell into an uneasy doze, and he woke, tired and unrefreshed, to yet another wasted day of apprehension and inability to concentrate.

By evening, he had had enough of it, and, determined not to endure another night like the previous one, he did a thing he rarely did—he took a sleeping-pill, and slept like the dead till past nine the following morning.

This was the Monday—Bank Holiday Monday—and he reflected, thankfully, that this was his last day of constant anxiety and fear of Rita's return. Tomorrow, Tuesday, would be an ordinary working day, at last, and the moment he got to the office he would phone Derek at work and tell him that Rita's luggage would shortly be on its way to Wimbledon. *Tell* him, not ask him; since she'd left Adrian of her own accord, her belongings were now Derek's responsibility again, not his.

It was Derek's secretary who answered the phone.

"Mr Langley? No, I'm afraid Mr Langley's not in this week. Can I give him a message when he returns?... Oh. Oh, I see. No, I'm afraid he didn't leave an address ... Mrs Langley hasn't been well, you know, and he's taken her for a short holiday by the sea. No, the South Coast, he told me ... a little place called Seaford, not far from Eastbourne...."

CHAPTER XXIII

Seaford!

Adrian slowly lowered the receiver back into its cradle and sat staring in front of him, utterly non-plussed.

What the hell were they doing in *Seaford*, of all places? And it couldn't possibly be coincidence, because Rita knew perfectly well where Peggy and Amelia had gone—why, she'd actually mentioned the place by name—hadn't she?—in that note she'd left? Adrian wished violently, now, that he hadn't so recklessly tossed the note away after a single reading. If only he could re-read it now, he might find in it some clue, some hint, as to what on earth was going on.

Because the more he thought about it, the more extraordinary it seemed. Rita had only a few days ago been claiming to be terrified of Amelia—had, indeed, in her final note, declared that it was fear of Amelia that was driving her from the flat. Surely, Seaford was the very last place in the whole world that she would choose to go to for a holiday?

If she had chosen?

Maybe it had been Derek's idea? Maybe he had some mysterious reason of his own for wanting to contact Peggy and/or Amelia? And yet another mysterious reason for wanting to drag Rita into it? Goodness knows, he was a mysterious enough fellow; his attitude to Rita had always seemed to Adrian a mystery—a combination of fierce possessiveness with a queer kind of indifference, exploding every now and then into black and bitter hatred.

And now he'd taken her off for a nice little convalescent holiday in Seaford, the very place where—according to her obsession—murder awaited her. Had he dragged her there by force? Or lured her there by the prospect of some sort of confrontation with Amelia which would dispel her delusions?

But how come he knew where Amelia was, when Adrian himself didn't? Had Peggy and Amelia, while neglecting to write to *him*, written to Derek instead? Or to Rita?

The whole thing was mad. Completely mad. He couldn't make any shadow of sense of it. He couldn't understand in the least degree what any of the four of them could possibly be up to. . . .

That's the trouble with being as selfish as you are, Adrian. . . . You end up not knowing anything at all, about any of us. . . .

Or something to that effect. The words, now buried deep under tea-leaves and orange-peel in Dorothy's dustbin, stabbed him with sudden, shocking force.

Because they were true, in a way. *If* he'd bothered to find out that Seaford address, instead of leaving it all to Peggy: *if* he'd actually listened to what Rita said about her fears, instead of dismissing it all as rubbish: *if* he'd troubled, as soon as she disappeared, to ring round her friends and relations to find out if she was all right. . . .

If . . . if . . . if. . . .

All right, so he was selfish. He knew he was—goodness knows enough people had told him so, particularly women. Selfish, and proud of it, he was accustomed to tell himself, because after all selfishness is the trendiest of all the failings; and it didn't, in Adrian's opinion, do half as much harm as the maudlin efforts of the do-gooders and the martyrs, for ever confusing every issue with their muddled, unforeseeable motivations.

With another of those flashes of visual recall, he saw before his eyes a further sentence from Rita's note:

You never think about other people, and so of course you never learn anything about them.

This did give pause for thought. As a scientist, he could not dismiss lightly a suggestion that, by his chosen life-style, he was actually blocking off access to data which is freely available to others—others far stupider than himself, too, and with less experience of the world. Like Dorothy, for instance. In his position, Dorothy would by now have known exactly what was going on in Seaford, and why. . . . Hell, maybe she *did*!

He rang her straightaway; but even down the telephone, and

even allowing for her devious partisanship, he could tell that she knew nothing. Nothing, that is, about this Seaford business; that she knew more than she would say about Rita's actual departure still seemed to him probable, but that was of no importance now.

He rang Rita's mother next; and various acquaintances in whom she might conceivably have confided her plans: but they were all either away, or knew nothing.

All day, in the intervals of work, he worried and puzzled over it, but no light dawned. The whole thing seemed completely crazy. And the most maddening, frustrating thing of all was that without the Seaford address of either of the two parties, there was nothing whatsoever that he could do. In his wilder moments, he thought of getting straight into his car and making for the place, and then, once there, simply to keep driving around in the hopes of seeing one or another of them in the street. But Seaford, though described by Derek's secretary as "a little place", wasn't all *that* little. He looked it up: Population 17,000. You could drive around for days and not run into the person you were looking for.

Oh, well. Maybe when he got home there'd be a letter? At least the posts were working again now.

But there wasn't. And there had been no phone calls. He had a long, unsatisfying talk with Dorothy, in the course of which he wormed out of her the fact that she *had* helped Rita to get away during his absence—"but only because I've got two eyes in my head, Mr Summers, and I could see how miserable you both were" —but Rita had told her nothing except that she was going back to her husband "and didn't want anyone to be told just yet".

Dorothy was repentant, and obviously much worried and concerned at this latest turn of events: she declared, tearfully, that she'd never forgive herself, and if the whole lot of them were lying there murdered in Seaford, then plainly it would be all her, Dorothy's fault.

Adrian did his best to assure her that they weren't, and it wouldn't; and finally went upstairs reflecting that if these were the rewards of listening attentively to another person's anxieties, then maybe he'd stay the way he was after all.

It was past nine by now; and he entered the flat with a vague hope that some clue, some message might have materialised in his absence: but of course it hadn't.

It *was* strange that Peggy had neither written nor phoned; and Amelia too. It was more than strange: it was extraordinary.

What proof have you that they ever *went* to Seaford?

—thus Rita had challenged him in her note; but it made no sense. If they *hadn't* gone, for whatever reason, then they'd certainly have let him know. And Amelia would have come on Sunday as usual— on both Sundays . . . it was nearly a fortnight now.

Was it just conceivable that there *had* been a letter from one or other of them, and he hadn't noticed it? If it had come fairly early on, before he'd begun worrying, and if, amid all the stresses and anxieties of his recent existence, he had just gathered it up with all his business correspondence and pushed it into a drawer somewhere?

He began going through his desk systematically, drawer by drawer.

At the third one down, he stopped. The sight of his yellow folder of press-cuttings stirred some memory at the back of his mind . . . a memory of something unfinished . . . an uneasiness . . . a reminder of some loose ends of some sort, somewhere. . . .

That was it! The diary! Amelia's silly, pathetic, love-lorn diary that he'd put away safely for her three—no, four—Sundays ago— the last Sunday before the accident. Had put it away here, just underneath this yellow folder—and now it was gone!

Had the child come and fetched it? No, of course she hadn't, she hadn't been here at all since that day—and anyway, she wouldn't know where to look. Hadn't she missed it, though, in all this time? Why hadn't she rung up and asked him about it? Naturally, she wouldn't have used the word "diary", and neither would he. An "exercise book with a red marbled cover" would have been the subject of their conversation throughout. They could trust each other, he and Amelia.

But she hadn't rung. She hadn't asked what had become of it. She couldn't have fetched it, because she didn't know where it was.

So who was there, besides himself, who *did* know where it was . . . ?

An icy chill went through him, right down his spine and trickling into every limb.

"It's my opinion you should report it to the headmistress immediately" . . . Rita's sharp, accusing voice was once more in his ears; it seemed to echo all about him in the empty flat, whispering from the walls, repeating and repeating itself in a jumbled medley as though from invisible loudspeakers everywhere: "The headmistress . . . the headmistress immediately. . . ." and he now knew suddenly, and without the smallest doubt, exactly what it was that had happened.

So Amelia *had* got a motive, just as Rita had kept telling him. Many a crime has been committed for a motive far less compelling.

But the crime, by now, meant nothing to him. It was the agony of humiliation, the insupportable shame that his little girl must have gone through beforehand, that held him rigid. Crouched over the open drawer, he literally could not move.

Not even when he heard footsteps crossing the room behind him —two sets of them, quite firm and distinct . . . no furtive tiptoeing this time.

It seemed like minutes, but could actually only have been a second or two before, from his ungainly crouching position, he managed to turn his head, and look at the two young people staring down at him. He had never seen either of them before. . . . Yes, he had; the sallow, overweight boy with the bad posture was the one Dorothy had hopefully pointed out to him as a possible new suitor for Kathy.

The girl spoke first. She was slim, and stood very straight, and with her blue eyes and waist-length fairish hair would have been very pretty if she hadn't been so angry.

"I'm Myra Owen," she announced herself fiercely; "and this is my husband. I'm not having him persecuted any longer! He's a marvellous teacher, and absolutely innocent, and we're not having him hounded out of his very first job and his whole career ruined by a pack of wicked lies! We've come to have it out with you, Mr Langley, once and for all!"

CHAPTER XXIV

"BUT MUMMY, I don't want to go out with them," protested Amelia. "And anyway, it's a horrible day."

It was, too. Outside the windows of the comfortable hotel lounge a thin, drizzling rain fell. The parade was gleaming with wet, and almost deserted; and beyond it the grey sea and the grey sky merged at the horizon into an off-putting expanse of nothingness.

Peggy, too, thought that Rita's invitation had been a tactless one. To telephone out of the blue like that, and—as Amelia had pointed out—on such a nasty day, to announce that she and Derek had arrived in Seaford and would very much like to take Amelia out—well, it put everyone in a spot. If Peggy refused on her daughter's behalf, it would simply look like mean-spirited jealousy: and if there was one thing that Peggy had kept clearly in mind throughout these four years of vicissitudes, it was her original resolution that she would *not*—absolutely *would not*, in any circumstances whatsoever display mean-spirited jealousy towards her ex-husband's mistress. She had seen other deserted wives behaving in such ways, and it never hurt the mistress the least little bit, whereas the cost of it to the wives in dignity, self-respect and pride was beyond all measuring.

So Amelia had *got* to go. Anything else would look like Peggy having dissuaded her.

"*Please*, darling—" she began; and then stopped, seeing the familiar, mulish look coming over her daughter's features for the first time this holiday. It was a shame; she'd so wanted this fortnight to be a happy, amicable time for the two of them, and so far it had been. She hated to introduce this note of discord; and yet it didn't seem such a *very* big thing to ask of the child—just one afternoon?

Of course, Peggy still had no inkling of Amelia's *special* reason for hating Rita—Amelia would never have dreamed of telling her mother about it—or, indeed, anyone else. Actually, that first white-hot agony of rage and humiliation had cooled considerably since Daphne had brought her back the diary, safe and sound, on the very day after the accident. Apparently it had been picked up by a fifth-former from the floor some feet away from where Rita had fallen, and from her, via various friends and sisters of friends, it had found its way into Daphne's hands, and she had brought it straight over. Since it looked from the outside so like an ordinary boring exercise book, there was every chance that no one in the motley chain of messengers would have read it; and if they had, they would never, ever dare admit to it, which comes to almost the same thing.

With the diary safe in her possession once more, Amelia naturally began to feel better; and when, as the days went by, no rumours came to her ears of a summons for Amelia Summers to go to the headmistress; no letter arrived for Mummy announcing that Amelia was to be expelled . . . well, bit by bit, naturally, her fears began to subside, and she came to the comfortable conclusion that Rita's accident must have occurred *before* she'd had a chance to show the thing to anybody, not after: a strange and marvellous mercy of Providence indeed.

But all the same, Amelia did not at all want to go out with Rita and Derek. Why should she? It was much nicer sitting here by the electric fire reading, or talking to Mummy. For some reason, she and Mummy had been getting on much better since they'd come down here; maybe it was because of having all these fellow-guests to giggle about? Real oddities some of them were, Mummy had been drawing caricatures of them, just like the old days at the dentist's, and Amelia had had a try, too, and discovered that she was really rather good. In secret, delicious intimacy behind one of the palms, they had whispered, and compared notes, leaning over one another's shoulders in fits of suppressed mirth, Mrs Oh-No-Darling vying for pride of place with Colonel That-Clock's-Slow.

It was fun, especially on a rainy afternoon like this. Why was Mummy going out of her way to spoil it all?

"You might at least have *asked* me," Amelia grumbled, with considerable show of justice. "How would *you* like it if someone accepted frightful invitations on *your* behalf, and then only told you when it was too late to get out of it? *I* know, though!"—her voice changed, became suddenly eager and animated. "I know! I'll run out to the car as soon as they arrived and explain to them that I'm *terribly* sorry, but I've already been invited to tea with the Oh-No-Darlings. It's not even a lie, you know, really; they *are* always inviting me because of Felicity Oh-No-Darling being such a wet, and they're trying to get her to make some nice friends. . . ."

Peggy shook her head despairingly. It wouldn't do. She couldn't possibly have sympathised more, but all the same, it just wouldn't. In no time at all it would be all round the neighbourhood that she, Peggy, had grudged her daughter a pleasant little outing with her future stepmother.

"Oh, Amelia, it's such a little thing," she pleaded. "Just one afternoon! Why must you be so obstinate . . . ?"

Dear oh dear! Real acrimony was creeping into the thing! And just when everything had been going so well between the two of them—and now it was all going to be spoiled!

Actual tears were welling up in Peggy's eyes; and in her despair she suddenly gave up, abandoned all her reasoned arguments, and threw her cards on the table.

"Don't you *see*, darling?" she wailed. "If you don't go, it'll look as if *I've* stopped you . . . that I'm jealous! Everyone'll think . . ."

And of course Amelia understood instantly. She knew all about humiliation, and pride, and having to keep your end up. She threw her arms round her mother's neck in instant, loving capitulation.

"Oh, Mummy, why didn't you say that before? *Of course* I'll go! I'll go up and get ready at once. . . ."

And a few minutes later, dressed in anorak, trousers, and old Wellington boots, she was climbing into the back seat of Derek's car. She hadn't really known what to wear, because Rita hadn't said what they were going to do, so she had prepared for the worst; and it appeared that she had been right. Rita, too, was wearing Wellingtons, and was all bundled up in a heavy fisherman-knit jersey, from the bulky collar of which her neck-brace protruded awkwardly. With this tough, out-doors sort of outfit she was wearing, rather incongruously, a glittering chain-belt of a bright gold colour, and she still had to carry a stick to lean on as she walked.

During the few minutes of polite conversation in the lounge, the afternoon's plans were divulged. They would be taking Amelia out to tea, of course, but first Rita was anxious for "a nice blow on the Downs" in her company. Derek would drive them up to a suitable spot, and pick them up afterwards, but he himself had set his heart on strolling along under the cliffs this afternoon looking for specimens of the Something-or-Other Seaweed. At this boring and specialised bit of information, Colonel That-Clock's-Slow woke suddenly and very surprisingly from his afternoon nap to reveal himself as a fellow seaweed enthusiast, and argumentative with it; and if it hadn't been for the fact that both the Langleys seemed quite inordinately keen on getting started with their dismal afternoon's programme, there is no knowing how boring the conversation would have become, or how long it would have gone on.

It was still drizzling, though perhaps not quite so hard, by the time Derek left them on the cliff-top; and though she had no special fondness for Derek—indeed she only knew him slightly—Amelia watched with longing as the car grew smaller and smaller in the distance, winding away down the steep, zig-zag road by which they had come.

Because the embarrassment of being left all on her own with Rita was awful. Why Rita had arranged—or allowed Derek to arrange—that this was the way it should be, Amelia could not imagine. Surely the whole thing was at least as embarrassing for Rita as it was for her? More so, if anything, Rita being as it were the guilty party in the case, the perpetrator of the original injuries.

For some minutes, they walked almost in silence, and very, very slowly because of Rita's lameness. She was leaning heavily on her stick at every step, and their Wellingtons squelched in the short, soaked turf. It was almost the only sound there was; on such an afternoon as this, there was no one to be seen for miles, and even the gulls seemed to have been silenced by the grey depressingness of the day.

Walking along like this, so very slowly, so very cautiously, through the soft, enveloping drizzle, was chilly work, and despite her lined anorak, Amelia began to shiver a little. There was no wind, but the all-pervading wetness of the salt-laden air had a curiously penetrating quality; it seeped through and past every garment you could pile on and got into your very bones. Amelia would have liked to have asked Rita to hurry up a bit, but of course you couldn't say such a thing to a person who was limping. She thought of offering her arm—but simultaneously with this came the thought of the physical contact involved, and she shrank away from it.

On they trailed, still with scarcely a word spoken. Amelia looked from the dim wastes of sea on their left to the bare, rain-swept curve of the Downs on their right, and wondered yet again what they were here for. Nothing but sporadic patches of leafless brambles broke the desolation of the view, and for someone in Rita's condition, with every step an obvious effort, the whole expedition seemed just plain crazy. And to choose as a companion Amelia, of all people, when the two of them had so much reason to hate each other!

An awful possibility crossed Amelia's mind. Had Rita brought her out here on her own in order to *apologise* to her? To try and make amends for the awful thing she had done, or tried to do? Was *this* why it had been arranged that Derek should tactfully take himself off—so that Rita and Amelia could have some hideous sort of tête-à-tête, with Rita apologising, and begging Amelia's forgiveness? Amelia's very soul squirmed at the thought of such a confrontation.

". . . as we forgive those that trespass against us . . ."

Yes, but what do the words actually *mean*? The thing that stands between an injured party and the one who has done the injuring is not something to which forgiveness can be applied like some sort of ointment. Forgiveness really doesn't come into it, for what stands between such a pair in actual fact is embarrassment: an embarrassment, in this case so vast, so intractable, that the words "I forgive you" or "I don't forgive you" would simply have no relevance.

A small, sharp cry from a little behind her roused Amelia to the fact that she had unwittingly outdistanced her slower-moving companion. She stopped at once, and turned to retrace her steps. Rita, she saw through the thick damp air, was now right on the cliff-edge, peering anxiously over.

Amelia quickened her pace.

"What is it?" she called; and Rita, gesturing down towards the cliff-face, replied:

"My belt! My chain-belt! Look, it's gone over the edge. It must have come undone somehow. Look!"

By now, Amelia had come alongside, and was looking over. Sure enough, on a ledge only about seven or eight feet below, lay the belt, coiled like a glittering snake against the chalk.

Amelia was an agile and enthusiastic climber. She could see that the ledge was fairly wide and solid-looking, that the distance was not great, and that there were convenient hand- and foot-holds at a variety of points. And the cliff, here near the top, was not even quite sheer.

"Don't worry; I'll get it for you," she said confidently, thankful to have something definite to do, to talk about, at last. "If you'll just stand back a bit, Rita, so I can get over. . . ."

The descent, as she had judged, was an easy one, though of course she had to be a bit careful about her rubber-soled boots on the wet, slippery chalk surfaces. In a matter of seconds, she was clutching the glittering gold links in triumph, and preparing for the return climb.

Above her, Rita's face was peering over anxiously. She seemed to be leaning over, in a crouching position, in a way that struck Amelia as slightly perilous, especially when you considered that heavy, clumsy contraption round her neck.

"It's all right. I've got it. You get back from the edge," she called; but Rita only leaned over yet further, still in that tense, purposeful attitude. And now Amelia noticed that the figure above had the walking-stick dangling from one hand; she was reaching over with it, poking and prodding vaguely in Amelia's direction.

"Take hold of it," she suggested fatuously, "I'll help pull you up."

"No, thanks," called back Amelia decisively. "I'm perfectly all right: it's easy."

And so it was—or would have been—if it hadn't been for that stick swaying and teetering about so annoyingly just above her face.

"I don't need it, Rita, honestly," Amelia called; and then, when Rita didn't seem to hear her, she shouted, with quite an edge on her voice:

"*Please*, Rita! Take it away, and get right back. It's only getting in my way—" as indeed it was, wobbling and wavering within an inch of her face, prodding and jabbing vaguely at every ledge and hand-hold as it came within reach.

"It's in my *way*, Rita!" she called again, loudly, and with just the beginnings of panic in her voice; but still the stick prodded and jabbed. Each time she reached her hand towards any convenient protuberance on the cliff-side, the stick would be there first, making it impossible for her to get a firm grip.

"Rita!" she shrieked, "Rita, stop it!" and above her, silhouetted against the grey, waterlogged sky, the head and the neck-brace, like a strange and uncouth bit of mediaeval machinery, leaned yet nearer. . . .

*   *   *

The "Mr Langley" hardly registered with Adrian at first. He was staring, dumbfounded, not at his blonde accuser with the flashing eyes, but at the round-shouldered youth who cringed nervously at her side.

So *this* was the wonderful, the incomparable "Mr Owen"! This shy, stooping, bespectacled youth without a word of say for himself, and who could not have been more than twenty-two! *This* was the being who had filled Amelia's dreams for all these months, the sun and moon around which her whole existence had revolved . . .! Adrian shook his head in a sort of bemused wonderment. What a thing is love!

"And it's no good shaking your head like that, Mr Langley!" the girl stormed on. "We *know* that you and your wife . . ."

It took till well after midnight to get it all sorted out, first in a stand-up row, and then, more calmly, over coffee; and finally, in a quite unforeseeable kind of intimacy, over white Cinzano. Gradually, between the three of them, they worked out what must have happened.

It had gone something like this.

Rita, true to her threats, had brought the diary to the school that afternoon and had presented herself at the headmistress's office, giving (as a general precaution against consequences to herself) a name that was neither her own nor Adrian's. But the subterfuge, as it turned out, defeated her whole purpose: the school secretary informed her, coldly, that in no circumstances could the headmistress discuss any child with anyone other than its own parent or guardian. Boiling over with frustration and anger, Rita had had to retire.

But there was still the unfortunate teacher himself. Maybe to confront him, personally, with the accusations would be an even better revenge, even more humiliating for the child whose very existence was wrecking Rita's partnership with Adrian, and against whom, in his doting paternal blindness, he would hear no evil word spoken?

He would hear some evil words now, all right—that is, if only this Mr Owen was still somewhere about the school. . . .

He was. Up in the art room by himself, as it happened, examining the preliminary sketches for the scenery of next term's production of *The Tempest*: and this strange woman had barged in on him, waving an exercise-book—a diary, she called it—and jabbering threats . . . accusing him of having seduced some girl . . . of the evidence being right here, in writing . . . and something about showing it to the headmistress. . . .

Young, inexperienced, in his very first job, Ronald Owen had panicked. He'd tried to snatch the book from Rita, to see what on earth was in it, but she was too quick for him; she had whipped it away, laughing, and darted through the door, still flinging threats and abuse over her shoulder . . . he had lunged after her, and in the brief and violent struggle at the head of the stairs, she had gone headlong down. He had heard from below the cries of all sorts of people rushing to her aid, and so had simply slunk away, hoping against hope that this might be the end of the matter.

But when, on the Friday, he saw that piece in the paper, all his fears returned. He did not doubt for one moment that the unnamed assailant to whom the victim so cryptically referred must be himself; and indeed, for all he knew, he *might* have pushed her. In that sort of struggle, there is no knowing who may have pushed whom.

At this point, not knowing which way to turn, he had confided in his wife, who (as Adrian had already noticed) was not one to let the grass grow under her feet.

Blackmail, Myra had diagnosed briskly; adding that now, after this unfortunate accident on the stairs, this evil woman would doubtless—as soon as she was well enough—be adding charges of attempted murder to her other threats; she would threaten to reveal that Ronald Owen had had, that afternoon, a most powerful motive for wanting to silence her.

But of course, all these threats and accusations would depend on one piece of evidence only—the diary, and whatever allegations it contained. Once get the diary out of her hands, and she wouldn't have a leg to stand on.

From the piece in the paper they knew her address, and her real name too.

So what were they waiting for?

If ever there was a case for justifiable housebreaking, this was it.

And in fact, housebreaking in the strict sense didn't come into it. Dorothy's slap-happy way of running her establishment, with doors left unlocked at all hours, and strange characters on the stairs gleefully accounted for as being someone or other's new boy friend or girl friend, would have been a boon to any intruder; and especially to these two, who had a long search ahead of them among all Adrian's accumulated books and papers. To complete it, they had to come over and over again, at times when Myra wasn't working, when Adrian wasn't at home, and when Dorothy wasn't up there gossiping with Rita. Rita herself wasn't much of an obstacle; while she sat or lay immobilised in one room, they could be concentrating on the other.

A professional burglar would doubtless consider that they had it made; and indeed, there was only one small obstacle standing between them and ultimate success: the diary wasn't in fact there.

By the time the whole story had been pieced together, and its various ramifications discussed at length between the three of them, it was very late indeed, and Adrian felt obliged to drive the young couple—they hadn't their own car yet—back to Gunnersbury. And afterwards, driving home alone through the deserted streets, his immediate feeling was the satisfying one of an evening well spent; of a mystery solved, of an uncomfortable burden lifted.

But as he drove on through the darkness, almost the only car left on the roads at this dead hour of three in the morning, the newer, and perhaps more urgent, mystery began to push itself once more into the forefront of his mind.

Seaford. Nothing in tonight's revelations had shed the smallest light on what was happening down there.

Or had happened. Or was about to happen.

Adrian clenched his teeth, and put his foot on the accelerator, hurtling through the quiet, suburban streets at a speed which must have roused to insomniac fury many an inoffensive citizen. Speed was necessary, he knew it, he could feel it in his bones. But speed where? In which direction? To what destination? And under pressure of what unimaginable deadline?

CHAPTER XXV

THE HEAD SILHOUETTED against the pallid, rain-washed sky looked circular and quite featureless from down here, like a black melon. It was impossible to gauge its expression. And still the stick prodded, wavered, found its direction, lost it again, like the searching stick of a blind man. And still Amelia could not believe that Rita was doing anything other than trying, with great stupidity and ineptitude, to help her up. Indeed, from the over-hanging black disk of the head, words to this effect kept emerging:

"Go on, Amelia! Take hold of it! Pull yourself up—I've got a good grip on it," came the voice, full now of a strange urgency; and each time Amelia tried to brush the stick away, back it came ... now in her face ... now tapping quite sharply against her knuckles. If she tried edging her way along the cliff to her left, it followed; towards the right, and there it was waiting for her. . . .

"Rita!" she cried out, with desperation in her voice now; and even while she pleaded, there came upon her the symptom dreaded by all climbers everywhere: her knees began to tremble ... her elbows too ... an uncontrollable jerking took command of every muscle, and it was impossible for her to move an inch in any direction. She dared not look up; even to climb down to the safety of the ledge only a couple of feet below was now beyond her power.

And as she clung there, paralysed by wave after wave of un-controllable terror, she became aware of some vast and extra-ordinary change coming over things: a sort of lurching of the air about her ... a mighty surge of movement. She was scarcely aware of having glanced momentarily upward, but graven on her retina was a lightning glimpse of Rita leaning closer and closer ... swooping towards her in a vast black curve, wings outspread, like the Angel of Death himself, blotting out the whole sky with darkness, and a mighty rush of wind.

For long, long seconds after Rita's body had smashed to pieces on the rocks below, Amelia still could not realise what had happened. The air still seemed to sway and heave with the passage of such a weight at such a speed, and she simply clung there, eyes tightly closed, unaware that the swooping as of great wings was over, that the huge shadow was no longer blotting out the light, and that the Angel of Death had gone on his way.

It must have been ten minutes or more before the shuddering of her limbs subsided sufficiently for her to climb down to the comparative safety of the ledge; and longer still before she found the strength to clamber up again, and heave herself over the cliff-edge to safety.

Of what followed afterwards, her memory was vague. She recalled looking wildly round for human help somewhere in the vast, darkening landscape of the Downs ... and then she remembered running, running, her face soaked with rain or with tears ... and then the cliff-road, and Derek waiting in the car, just as had been arranged. ...

To the kindly police officer who questioned her later that evening, Amelia explained as well as she could exactly what had happened. How Rita's chain-belt had fallen over the cliff-edge ... how she, Amelia, had climbed down to get it for her ... and how Rita, leaning over to see how she was getting on, must have leaned a little too far. But about that stick, probing and jabbing, she could not bring herself to speak, or even to think. And why should she? Rita was dead now. It was all over.

It did not occur to her—after all, she was only thirteen—that when two people go off alone together on to a solitary cliff, and only one of them returns alive, there is bound to linger afterwards, in some minds, a tiny flicker of suspicion. Still less did it occur to her that one of those minds might be that of her own beloved father.

For he, and he alone, knew what cause she had to hate Rita.

"I *told* you so!" he might hear the dead Rita's insidious voice whispering to him, in uneasy dreams, for many a year to come: "Didn't I *warn* you ...?"

Might have heard it, that is, if it hadn't so happened that Rita's handbag had been found, more or less intact, not many yards from where she fell. In it were found four letters. Three of them were letters written by Amelia and Peggy to Adrian some days ago, and intercepted by Rita, conveniently alone in the flat when the post came. The fourth one, also addressed to Adrian, had been written by Rita herself; it was stamped, sealed and addressed all ready for posting. If all had gone according to plan, he would have received it, probably, the following morning. As things were, the police handed it over to him some hours earlier, and this is what he read:

My dear, dear Adrian,

You will have heard by now the terrible, terrible news. I know how bitterly you will feel the loss of your daughter, and God forbid that anything *I* say should make it harder for you. But all the same, I feel I must tell you the truth. I will tell it no one else, only to you; and after this I will never speak of it again.

As you will know by now, the poor child's death has been accepted as an ordinary accident. But, Adrian, I have to tell you it *wasn't* an ordinary accident. Have they told you yet that when they found her, my chain-belt was clutched in her hand? And that near by lay my walking-stick, which she snatched away when she attacked me?

Yes, attacked me. I'm sorry, Adrian, I know this will hurt, but I have to tell you. She tried to take me by surprise as I stood with my back to her, gazing at the sea, but some instinct somehow made me turn round just in time. . . .

It only lasted a few seconds. She pulled and dragged me towards the edge, she snatched my stick from me to upset my balance . . . and then, all in a moment, as we struggled, my chain-belt gave way, and over she went. I tried to save her, Adrian, even at the risk of being dragged over with her . . . but it all happened too quickly . . . she was gone.

Oh, Adrian, Adrian, I don't want to seem to be reproaching you at such a time as this—but oh, if only you'd *listened* to me! If only you'd paid attention to my warnings, then the poor child would by now have been in some suitable place where they'd have taken proper care of her, and this dreadful tragedy need never have happened.

But this is no time, my darling, for useless regrets. What's done is done, and at least you still have *me*—the one person who will never leave you, never let you down, and who will devote her life to trying to make you happy again.

I love you, Adrian: I love you.

Rita.

Although he already knew the true facts, Adrian, as he read, was nevertheless filled with a horrible fear—a sort of nightmare preview of how he would have felt if this letter had reached him *before* he knew that Amelia was safe; *before* Peggy had rung to say that they would be on their way back to London on the next train.

It was unendurable. It was beyond imagining. Adrian deliberately blotted it from his consciousness, and read the letter through a second time, more calmly.

In all this evil and malevolent farrago of treachery and lying, one sentence shone out as the truth, clear and unmistakable: "I love you".

She had, too. That's what it had all been about.

In her own, special way, she *had* loved him: and he had known it. But what could he have done?

CHAPTER XXVI

A MONTH HAD passed, and it was May. The lilacs were out now in Dorothy's bit of back garden, and with the scent of them floating through the open kitchen window, Dorothy sat polishing up the gilt clasps of her grandmother's old diary in readiness for a very special session with it this evening.

Though she had tried not to show it too much at the time, Dorothy had been much disappointed by Amelia Summers' reaction to the heirloom. Instead of showing a proper interest in all the titled persons therein mentioned—Lady Rochford, the Honourable Ralph and the rest—the child had simply kept asking question after question about that wretched curate who had married a Miss Overton—not an actual member of the family at all, but merely a governess. Most disappointing.

But this time, it was going to be different. In fact, life looked like being somewhat different altogether from now on, because this very week a new and most aristocratic lodger had arrived—a baronet, or so he said—who was willing to take over the Squatters' Flat exactly as it was, and put it to rights himself. And though he was obviously quite elderly—his little pointed beard was almost white, and so was his sparse hair—it really looked as if he might be going to make good his promise. Already, he had fixed the dripping tap in Dorothy's bathroom, and had nailed down a loose floorboard for her. Dorothy had had no idea that baronets could be so handy; or indeed, so willing to rent rooms with the plaster falling down and the window-frames splintered. But this particular baronet, it seemed, had fallen on hard times; and though, of course, most baronets these days have fallen on hard times, Sir Montague apparently laboured under the additional misfortune of having had a spell in a mental hospital, from which he had only recently been discharged. This was liable to put most landladies against him— but not, of course, Dorothy, who welcomed him with open arms. His little weakness (she explained, in strictest confidence, to anyone who would listen) was that every so often he would barricade himself into his room imagining that the Russians were after him:

but, as Dorothy pointed out to her less than enthusiastic household, it wasn't really much of a problem: after all, either the Russians *were* after him or they weren't; and if they weren't, then there was nothing to worry about; and if they were, then it proved that he wasn't mad after all; so either way it all worked out for the best. Against which unassailable logic, there seemed nothing more to be said.

Anyway, it was all very exciting, and, Dorothy reflected, Sir Montague *must* be a real baronet—or at least something of the sort—because he'd shown such a very intelligent interest in this Amelia Ponsonby diary—one of *the* Ponsonbys, you know—and had seemed to know of, or be descended from, or in some way connected with, almost every one of the august personages who featured in its pages. This very evening, he was going to go through it properly with her, and help her construct a family tree similar to his own.

Oh, Posterity, Posterity!

They *are* keeping faith with you, Amelia Caroline Ponsonby, after their fashion.

*   *   *

And what of Amelia Summers? The new term had begun now, of course—she'd been back at school nearly a fortnight—and right now her friends were condoling with her because, having been away at the end of last term, she'd failed to put her name down on the list for the Keats's house trip with Mr Owen tomorrow.

Amelia was responding with the appropriate groans and despairs that were expected of her; but somehow, deep in her heart, she didn't really mind all that much. She had decided this term that history, not English, was her favourite subject: only this morning, Mr Everard had read out her essay on "Education in the Victorian Era" to the whole class, pronouncing it "very thoughtful and well-written", handing it back to her with one of those nice smiles that quite transformed his grave, rather stern features.

Of course, she didn't reveal any of this to her companions. For one thing, it would have led to such a spate of questions and excited exclamations, and Amelia felt that she had had enough of questions and excited exclamations to last her a lifetime. Because, of course, for the first few days of term, everyone had been wild with curiosity to hear about the "South Coast Cliff Tragedy" which had been in all the papers during the holidays; and Amelia, who usually so enjoyed being the centre of attention, had found that she hated having to talk about it, and was deeply thankful that the subject seemed at last to be closed.

The police enquiries down at Seaford were closed, too. Indeed, the discovery of Rita's bag, with its irrefutable proof of her own intent to murder, had more or less put a stop to further speculation or suspicion.

Indeed, who was there to suspect? Amelia was obviously in the clear now, after the discovery of that carefully pre-arranged letter, and Rita was revealed as unquestionably the villain of the piece. The only remaining mystery concerned her precise motive.

Had she really been frightened of Amelia? Or had she merely been afraid of the consequences of her lying accusations when the time inevitably came for them to be compared with Amelia's own account of what had happened? And if the latter, then had all those terrors and delusions about Amelia creeping around the flat been merely an elaborate bit of play-acting, designed to lend verisimilitude to the story she planned to tell about the murder itself?

Or had it, perhaps, *begun* as a bit of play-acting; but then, later, when she actually *did* hear furtive footsteps creeping around, while she lay there helpless and alone . . .?

There was only one person who might conceivably know the answers to these questions, and that was Derek. It was Derek who had been with Rita during the last days of her life, and it was just possible that, if she'd been genuinely frightened, she might have confided in him.

But Derek wasn't talking. And indeed, why should he? After all, if he went around discussing his wife's possible motives, it wouldn't be long before someone, somewhere, began to wonder if he hadn't perhaps guessed what was in her mind when she set off across the cliffs with Amelia that afternoon? And if he *had* guessed, then might it not further have occurred to him that anyone planning to push another person over a cliff will be obliged, at some point in the proceedings to come very, very near to the cliff-edge themselves; so near, indeed, and in such a preoccupied state of mind, that a third party, who has been creeping along behind at a safe distance ... dodging down among the blackberry clumps when necessary, and watching for his moment ...?

But how *could* Derek have been following along behind? He'd been far below on the beach, strolling along *under* the cliffs, looking for that special seaweed whose name no one had bothered to remember. Not that anyone had actually *seen* him searching for the stuff, but half a dozen people at least had heard him declaring his intention to spend the afternoon thus—and anyway, it was so exactly what he *would* do, so completely in character. In addition to which, he'd actually had some specimens of seaweed in his rucksack when he got back, all ready to show to anyone who was interested, not excluding the police. As it happened, the one person who *might* have been interested—old Colonel That-Clock's-Slow—was asleep in his chair throughout, and no one—least of all Derek—had any inclination to rouse him.

And it never occurred to the police—indeed, why should it?—to examine the film Derek brought back in his camera that afternoon, as well as the specimens he brought back in his rucksack. And even if they had—even if Derek had actually boasted to them about the marvellous shots he'd got of Ophrys sphegodes (the slides of which were destined to be his prize exhibit at the September meeting of the Dorset and Hampshire Botanical Society)—even if he'd expatiated at length on how uncommon it was, and how it had never been found in just this area before—even then, how likely was it that any of his hearers would have known that Ophrys sphegodes is the botanical name for the rare and beautiful Spider-Orchid? And that the Spider-Orchid couldn't, by any possibility at all, have been found during a stroll along the base of the cliffs, but only on top, growing in the light, chalky turf, far, far above the sea?